The Witch and the Ostrich

The Witch and the Ostrich

Jordan A. Werner

Copyright © 2023 by Jordan A. Werner

All rights reserved. No part of this publication may be reproduced, distributed or transmitted in any form or by any means, without prior written permission.

Space Wizard Science Fantasy
Raleigh, NC
www.spacewizardsciencefantasy.com

Publisher's Note: This is a work of fiction. Names, characters, places, and incidents are a product of the author's imagination. Locales and public names are sometimes used for atmospheric purposes. Any resemblance to actual people, living or dead, or to businesses, companies, events, institutions, or locales is completely coincidental.

Cover Design by MoorBooks
Editing by Heather Tracy
Book Layout © 2015 BookDesignTemplates.com

The Witch and the Ostrich/Jordan A. Werner.— 1st ed.
ISBN 978-1-960247-18-6

Author's website: https://jwernerwrites.wordpress.com/

To my parents, who spared my life after I switched my major from Biopsychology to Film and Media.

And my sister, who went through one of the later drafts. Sorry you had to read all that shite.

CONTENTS

Quin and Fergus

A rag-wearing highwayman lay dead half a mile down the road from the lonely boondock rail station Quin and Fergus had just arrived from. Bits of smashed skull and brainy pulp formed a halo around where the rest of his head used to be. His killer—an eight-foot-tall, dark-plumed, black-eyed ostrich—hummed a tune Quin figured was supposed to be some kind of necromantic spell. He conducted the air with a baton fashioned from bone which he held with his beak. Except the only sound coming out of Fergus's absurdly long, salmon-colored neck was a high-pitched whining. Wherever the highwayman's soul was now, she had a feeling a crooning ostrich wasn't terribly likely to coax it back.

"Ferg, it didn't work the first dozen times you tried it, it's not gonna start working now," Quin told him as she searched a second dead highwayman's rightmost trouser pocket. Empty.

The two sorry morons had jumped out of from behind a pair of thick-trunked dead trees, armed with—god bless them—bread knives. Their bare pockets attested to just how effective that had been. Though, Quin supposed it could've also meant they were the first saps these two had run into. She'd be surprised if there were lots of people heading down to Queensworth, or up to the station. Queensworth was, by repute, something of a pit. When they arrived, she hadn't seen a single person waiting at the station apart from its solitary station agent.

Fergus gave up, prodded the dead highwayman with his enormous ostrich toe and tucked his baton back into his generous plumage. *You never know. A man can dream,* he said. His "voice" rattled around in her skull and sounded exactly how a telepathic necromancer ostrich ought to sound.

"Right. So what exactly would you do with him if you *did* manage to resurrect him?"

Hurm. Have him carry my things, do a silly dance, something or other. Whatever will distract me from the fact that I've found myself protecting you on some errand for the Stardust *out in the middle of an Incolf backwater for what feels like the third time this year.*

Quin held up two fingers. "Couple things. First off." One particular finger down. "Don't need you guarding me. At all. Second." She flicked that finger back and forth between the two of them. "This 'errand' is what's paying both our rents. You know, that thing you like to avoid contributing to? That makes sure the two of us don't wind up living out of some sewer in downtown Basdolon? Ringing any bells up there?"

Fergus preened himself, nipping at his shiny black feathers with his charcoal-grey beak. *You know,* he said, ignoring her reproach, *you should stick this in your writeup.* He nudged the corpse with his foot. *Might add a nice skosh of flavor to your review. A little gory apéritif, if you will.*

Quin whipped out her notepad and pencil from the front pocket of her red leather jacket and scribbled a few notes, mumbling them aloud as she jotted them down in longhand. "Dimwits ... bread knives ... both dead ... one tripped ... Fergus kicked other ... failed resurrection ... outside of ...

Queensworth ... on way ... to ... Crescent." She signed off on the last word with a flourish and a smirk.

Well, don't put that *part in!* Fergus complained as he finished preening. He shook himself, jostling the abundant leather and canvas pouches slung all over him with cords of hempen rope. They made him look a one-man...one-*bird*, flea market. Wands, totems, talismans, necklaces, and other enchanted thingies poked out of the pouches. Some were actual thingies. Like, penises. An eclectic variety of them, too. Hooked, barbed, curved, erect, flaccid. Fake, real. Cooked, sometimes pickled, all adorning his plumage. God only knew what he was going to use those for or where he'd even gotten them from. Quin had never asked and didn't intend to anytime soon.

"Which part?" she asked.

The failed resurrection part, obviously. Do you want our enemies to know I'm effectively de-beaked? Powerless? Neutered!

"Which enemies are we talking about here?" Quin pretended to idly count off on her fingers.

Laisona Magicks Incorporated, just for starters. No-good lying dunderheads, all of them.

"Why? Because they wrote you a bad review?" Fergus was always getting the absolute crap kicked out of him in the Letters to the Editor section of *The Daily Stardust,* where he advertised his services. He liked to insist his regular corner-page thrashings spoke to his productivity as a freelance practitioner of the mystic arts. Quin thought it cemented how shit of a wizard he was.

Bad review? Bad review? *They slandered me!*

"That's 'libeled,'" she said.

Fergus bristled. *You know Quin, back when I was Death Lord of Jocrom—*

Quin groaned. "Please. Regale me once more."

—I had people strung up by their innards for far less than mere pedantry. Innards, Quin! Have you ever tried suspending anything from anywhere with guts and viscera? It's slippery. Takes hours.

"I'm shaking," Quin said. "Laisona Magicks, Laisona Magicks..." She tasted the name on her tongue a few times, trying to remember where she'd heard it before. She snapped her fingers when it came back to her: "Are they the people whose warehouse you blew up?"

Fergus wilted, sheepish. *Ah, no. No, that was Dayzona Arcanics.*

"Then what'd you do with these other people?"

I didn't do any—

"Wait, weren't they the ones whose cows got eaten by that freaky mutant worm? You know, the one with the spikes?" she asked as she wiggled her fingers above her head.

Fergus looked away with an exasperated twitch, annoyance blooming on his face—so far as it could on a bird's.

...Yes.

"Ha! That was you?"

Well, I wasn't the worm, obviously.

"Yeah, I know. I'm saying that was your fault?"

No comment. But now you see why people can't know I am unable to raise corpses to do my bidding! Considering my recent string of...snafus, my necromantic prowess and its considerable reputation is the only thing keeping me marketable. Good god Quin, direct that thick melon of yours toward something other than work for once.

"Right, right. I'm so, ever so sorry," she intoned, throwing an "up yours" at Fergus the moment he looked away. She came close to asking him what he was going to do once someone *did* call on him for his necromantic prowess (so-called), and decided she'd rather zip her lip and watch that little disaster unfold naturally whenever it came 'round.

As she kicked the second corpse onto its front to check for any back pockets she could rifle through, Quin noticed a mark on the back of the man's neck, right at the base of his shaved skull: a raised sickle-shaped brand. She knelt to get a better look at it and whistled as she recognized their destination's logo. "Huh." Quin scanned the corpse with new insight. "Hey Fergus. These may not be highwaymen. See this?"

He keeled low to get a better look. *No!* Fergus scoffed, letting out a strangled wheezing sound that was probably a laugh. *This thin string of gristle, a Crescent gladiator? Fighting with, what, a breadknife? Ha! Poor twit wouldn't have lasted ten seconds in the Entraillion.*

Quin gestured toward the other corpse. "Go check the other one, see if he has the same mark."

Why?

"Just do it."

Bah! Fergus huffed. *I don't take orders from the likes of you, Quin.*

"Likes of what? Witches?"

Well, women. But tautologies and all.

Quin suppressed a snort. "Dick."

He glanced back at the other body. *Besides. Assuming he was branded in the same place, well, he doesn't have much neck anymore for me to check. Anyhow. Say he did. So what?*

"Because I'm thinking this means there's a bad review in the offing," Quin said, rubbing her hands eagerly.

Fergus cocked his head at her. *You're going to have to tell me how you reached that particular conclusion just from the ink on his scruff.*

"Well, it's weird they'd be all the way out here, for one thing. We've still got another five miles before Queensworth and the Crescent."

I don't see why that makes their being here odd. Perhaps they were looking for some spare coinage to supplement their combat pay.

Quin gave him a look, and while keeping eye contact, picked up the closest bread knife, waved it at him, then tossed it into the creek. It clanged against a rock and splashed into the meager eastward-trickling stream.

Fergus blinked. *And, pray tell, what exact inference was I supposed to divine from that?*

"You literally just said these guys wouldn't last a minute back home, why would they do any better in Queensworth? Again, big question is: Why are they all the way out here? Five miles from home?"

I just said why they'd be. As you graciously pointed out.

"Yeah, but if they were doing decently as gladiators at all, then they wouldn't need to be out here mugging. I think these two *escaped* the Crescent." She pointed toward the train station. "I'm betting they were hoping to get some coin off of us to afford tickets. If guys like these are all the arena has to speak for, then I've got a feeling the show's probably not gonna be anything spectacular."

And I was supposed to reach this conclusion from you waving a cooking implement in my face?

"Bread knifes are for baking, Fergus." She put on an imitation of his so-called voice: "Good *god,* use your tiny little brain for something other than work for once. I didn't shrink it down *that* much."

Well, pardon me for breathing, your witchiness. He made a haughty clucking noise. *Perhaps they hoped to stumble upon some poor unfortunate travelers such as us, steal our valuables, then sell them off to afford better armaments? Besides, didn't Jack already say the Crescent might be lower on the quality scale as far as arenas go?*

Of course, Fergus couldn't admit he was wrong. It was like trying to convince an art critic that a painting of a tree was just a painting of a tree, and not a metaphor for the current state of political discourse or whatever bullshit.

Then again, Jack—the *Stardust's* editor-in-chief—did say that bit about the Crescent being kinda shit, as a matter of fact. And as much as she wanted to be the correct one here, while still keeping an open mind for the sake of an objective review, Quin couldn't help but feel a spark of excitement at the prospect of getting to trash the Crescent. Negative reviews were always fun to write and sold a lot more papers than a middling review, or even a good one. It was basic human nature to enjoy seeing someone else getting themselves ripped a new asshole. Ergo, gladiatorial combat.

A dangerous glint flashed across one of Fergus's opaque onyx eyes. *You know...*

She knew that look too damn well. "Ferg, what're you plotting, and why am I going to hate it?" Whenever Fergus got ideas, people tended to wind up dead, deadlines got missed, and she had to clean up whatever black-feathered mess got left behind. Entertaining as the chaos could be, the long-legged bastard was leagues more trouble than he was worth. In hindsight, she regretted turning him into an ostrich in the first place. Quite a bit.

But it wasn't like she could take the spell back, a fact she made sure to keep him perpetually unaware of. Hence his following her around: to make sure his one chance of returning to human form didn't kick the bucket. He'd never said as much, but he didn't have to.

If they're truly that poorly equipped, I could enter the games, Fergus proposed. *I'll win a few rounds, rake in the profits and install terror in the eyes of the popul—*

"Instill," Quin corrected him. He glared. "What?"

Hmph. Instill *terror in the eyes of the populace, thus proving myself as the most powerful, rich, terrifying warrior in Queensworth, at which point I establish a totalitarian regime in my image. From there, I will conquer the land using an army of vicious killers and animals, all liberated from the Crescent. And if you restore my human form, I will allow you to govern by my side as co-ruler.*

"So, what, you'll be mayor then? And what'd that make me, your secretary? Like hell."

I'll adjust our titles. Then afterward, we can begin plotting how to topple Her Dimwittedness and your fellow beldams.

She had no idea what establishing a regime in "his image" was supposed to entail and didn't care enough to ask. Same with what a beldam was, though since he was referring to the other Witches, she doubted it was anything complimentary. "Or. *Or,* you could use this as an opportunity to show off your magnificent gams and find yourself a girlfriend in the crowd," Quin said. "Half the effort, twice the fun."

Quin, please. Let's entertain serious *ideas here.* The way he said it, Quin was only half-sure he was aware of just how ludicrous his plan was. Fergus looked down at his legs, like he was checking to make sure they were still there. He looked up at her with what might have been a pout. *Hm. Besides, don't flatter yourself. My legs are hardly fetching.* He ruffled himself again. *So. Your thoughts?*

Quin made a whole show of mulling it over, puckering her lips and tapping a finger to her chin. Set an evil-overlord-turned-ostrich to rampage through a gladiatorial colosseum? Of course not! What a horrible, irresponsible idea!

Really though? She was pretty inclined. Mostly because the prospect of Fergus getting himself violently and hilariously disemboweled in front of a cheering crowd of thousands—with onlookers decorating his corpse with thrown bits of roasted corn kernels and small candies—was downright mouthwatering. Now *that* would make for a damned good illustration to accompany her review, with the added bonus of Fergus finally being out of her hair. She wondered if Her Majesty's stupid contract had a clause for *that.*

Then again. Conflicts of interest and all that. Jack would kill the article, seeing as how Fergus was something of a *Stardust* mascot by this point. Quin wasn't keen on being on the receiving end of any accusations of bias, or worse, blundering her assignment. Having been relegated to arena critic was bad enough. The next step down from there was traffic reporter. And that was on the optimistic side. She hadn't been joking before about the danger of winding up in a Basdolonian sewer.

"Hmm. I guess we could at least *check* about maybe registering you," she said, in a faux long-suffering tone.

Splendid! Then let us be on our way and let the wolves come and address their dinner. Mind your gun. Fergus continued on down the highway, waggling his tail-feathers back and forth as he strutted along. He scanned the area for new threats, giving Quin the impression of a feathery periscope with a paranoid operator.

Her gun. Right. Where'd she put it? She looked around for it. Whoop! There it was. She'd left it to rest against a tree, next to her rucksack with the few days' worth of clothes in it and a few snacks.

Quin gingerly recovered the four-foot-long musket. Engraved, oiled wood whispered against the rough, cracked rawhide of her fingerless gloves. She slipped it into the leather harness she wore over her jacket and picked the pack up by its strap.

She was about to tail after Fergus when something shifted at the corner of her eye. The breeze had flittered the corner of a folded-up piece of yellowed parchment sticking out of—what did you know—the back pocket of the trousers on Fergus's kill. Curious, she knelt, extracted the paper and unfolded it. The crudely drawn letters had been penned in dark-brown, smudged ink.

Fergus stopped at the crest of the creek-spanning stone bridge he was crossing and glowered at her impatiently. *Are you coming or not, woman?* he called. Not for the first time, she wondered whether he needed to raise his voice because he was at a distance, or if it was just something he did to make himself feel as though he had a real voice. Or to annoy her.

"I'll catch up," she called back.

You found something?

"Might've."

Well, don't take too long. We have places to be. Besides, I believe we're getting close to town! There's a faint fragrance of feces on the wind. He continued on.

As Quin unfolded the paper, she noticed the blotted brown spots, and realized it wasn't ink. Dried blood. She felt her heart skip a beat as she read it:

HELP. THE WITCH OF BASDOLON HAS SENT ME TO THE CRESCENT TO DIE. SEND HELP. BEN MEDINA.

Quin read it over once more to make sure she hadn't misread it. Ben Medina. Ben bloody Medina. Well, *shit.*

Quin paled. Oh, *shit.* Had she...Quin quickly checked the corpse and breathed a sigh of relief. It was too tall to have been Ben. Same with the other corpse.

Back when she'd first started up with *The Daily Stardust* about six years back, she'd done a puff piece on Ben Medina. He'd been the first Minister of Foreign Communications who hadn't been born in Basdolon, Incolf's capital, so the *Stardust* had been eager to get his words to print, seeing as how the other papers wouldn't so much as touch him with the business end of a broomstick. The interview hadn't made much of a splash. And truth be told, Medina hadn't been all that compelling. Your standard mousy civil servant.

Then he'd gone missing about a month ago. His disappearance received a likewise cool reaction, seeing as he'd never been particularly popular and had no family to worry on his behalf. Catherine from a floor down had buried the story somewhere in the corner of page ten for their weekday edition.

And the Witch of Basdolon...

Part of her had to wilt a little, because she knew the note wasn't referring to her. She didn't have the kind of power and infamy to earn a title like that. Not yet at least.

No, he was talking about Esder, that skinny, stuck-up, scary-as-all-fuck, satin-wearing *bitch*. Also, Quin's immediate senior among the Five. All of whom were bound by vows both political and magical not to get directly involved in governmental goings-on. Just to serve the Queen and her family when called upon—for all the sense that made as far as the whole no-politicking stipulation went.

So, if Esder had gone and sent a civil servant to die in a gladiatorial pit...

Quin salivated. If this note was genuine, that'd be a story. Fuck, that'd be *journalism*. The kind that could get her back to writing real articles for the *Stardust*. Articles paying more than portions of the rent. Articles that got certain powerful people—like a certain witch who'd reduced more than a few cities to rubble—in a heapload of shit.

Quin! Fergus shouted at her from what sounded like the other side of the bridge. *Don't make me double back. I tire of your lollygagging and all this walking.*

"Yeah, yeah," Quin said, smiling as she stuffed the slip of paper into her back pocket. Her fingers started twitching, eager for the feel of typewriter keys clacking beneath them. She caught up to Fergus, and they trotted onward to Queensworth. Quin had to fight herself from putting a little skip in her stride.

Going Nowhere Fast

The Soltan, draped in layers of thick woolen blankets, sat upon his gilded gold throne, the Seat of all Seats, which was fashioned quite splendidly to resemble a series of bodies stacked upon one another, their faces and limbs contorted in violent bliss. It sat upon a foot-high marble plinth, which afforded the Soltan a good view of the gargantuan antechamber in which he held court, with its gilded arches and the intricately patterned floral recesses in the walls, all trimmed with gold.

The main attraction was, of course, the set of three-story stained-glass windows that depicted his family's conquest of Jocrom. It showed seven Basdolonian figures, his ancestors, descending upon the country when it had been called Zha'kram, swords held high, repelling the natives in glorious battle. Those who had yet to fall and join the mounds of corpses beneath his family's feet retreated behind the meagre walls of Harashin, the capital. *His* capital, now.

Beside the Soltan prattled a man with a thick black beard who was draped in patterned and bejeweled finery, reading off a long, unraveled scroll that drooped to the floor. The man rerolled the scroll and bowed. "Your response to the diwan, sire?"

The Soltan shuddered and let out a pleased sigh. Then he sniffed. "Hm? Sorry, I wasn't listening. What was the issue again? Oh, and kneel, would you?"

The fop—Ehsan or something—knelt and said, "Apologies, Your Greatness. Your subjects in

Tosfhan. They request immediate aid, for fear that their central bank will collapse and send the middle classes into steep poverty. The diwan requests your command. What shall it be?"

"Oh, yes. What to do. Well. Hm. I'm not sure. It's just, finances, you know. Or work in general. Gives me the hives and such. I'm not sure." He lifted one blanket. "What would you suggest?"

There was a pause. A tan-skinned right hand emerged from the dark and began to speak, a beak of fingers flapping against a pointed chin-thumb. "Well, a solid first step would be to establish a regulatory agency," said a high nasal voice. "Set up an office in Tosfhan. Supervision is key. Think of the bank as the cookie jar and the borrowers as the naughty children. Do *not* allow interest rates to skyrocket. That's just asking for trouble. Once that's done, have your regulators compose a solid crisis management plan, just in case. And you're golden."

The Soltan nodded like he understood what any of that meant. "Hm, hm. I see. Would you agree?"

A pale hand emerged from beneath the blanket to give a thumbs-up before pulling its neighbor back inside.

"Very good, carry on then," the Soltan said. He let the blanket drop into his lap, leaned back and let out a satisfied exhale. "Aah. I do love a good session of campaigning."

"Politicking," said a woman's voice.

"Excuse me?" The Soltan looked around and discovered an ugly, red-furred and squat-nosed bat glaring up at him from the armrest of The Seat of all Seats.

"It's called *politicking,* idiot," the bat twittered in a husky voice with a faint trace of a strange accent to it. "Campaigning is when, you know, you run for political office. But I guess you wouldn't, seeing as when you announced the country's first set of elections since your inbred fuckwad ancestors showed up here, you literally buried the entire political opposition under a mountain of shit."

The Soltan shrugged. "It was a perfectly good excuse to demonstrate to my spymasters just how useless they were. And it unclogged the sewers." He pointed to the bat. "Ehsir or whatever, when you have a second, would you go and kill this..."

Eh-something-or-other was gone. In his place was a thick, towering flagpole holding aloft the tattered standard of his family, a skull with purple diamonds for eyes. Around it was curled a graceful blue wyvern the size of a bear. It stared down at him with dark pool eyes, its gnashing teeth throwing sparks all over his palace's reflective gold floors.

"I vote execution," the wyvern said in a hiss carrying a vaguely sarcastic tune, craning her head toward the flag. With just the barest of whispers, it set the standard alight. The Soltan watched as the fabric slowly burned away, turning to flame-winged butterflies before fading away into a growing gloom.

The Soltan swallowed. "Ah...I w-wasn't aware that a vuh-vote had been cast...who were...what are...who's the offender in question?" Darkness settled, and the only light came from the wyvern's glowing eyes, casting hot, pale light upon him. Then the windows blew apart in a shower of multicolored glass, letting in a pallid orange glow from outside. Something outside was on fire. Many things. A smell of cooking meat wafted in.

"As appealing as that is…" A barn owl swooped in and landed on the wyvern's head before proceeding to preen its curiously yellow feathers. "And as much as I'd love to see you let loose, darling, Her Majesty's wishes stand. He's coming back with us to Basdolon."

The Soltan shot to his feet in a panic, and the blankets fell to the floor, exposing his perfectly pedicured toenails. The wyvern growled in disgust at the sight of them. "Pastels."

"You're all, you're all idiots!" A black-feathered shrike with red eyes circled above his head, then swooped in at him. The Soltan ducked, but instead of diving at him and trying to peck his eyes out, it settled on the arm of his chair. "Forget the Queen, forget revenge. We're dragging this, this, this *accumulation* of venereal diseases out of here and planting him in front of a judge. A Jocromite judge. Then we're going to, we're going to put him before the people to do with him as they will. That's the only way to make this country whole again. Make its *people* whole again."

"Yeah, and while we're at it, we can establish free elections and give out candy to everyone who lines up for the ballot box," snickered the bat. "Good God, five hundred years and you're still this naive?"

"I don't, I don't take criticism from stupid children who can barely so much as, so much as vanish a building without turning to dust!" the shrike screeched.

The bat cackled. "That's amazing, you're so fucking old you think being seventy-one makes you a kid."

"Silence," the wyvern hissed.

The shrike began to curse out the bat, which nipped back at the shrike, then the two of them were flying at each other, clawing with talons and biting. The owl swooped between them to break up the fight, while the wyvern watched impassively, white flames reaching desperately out from behind the razor-sharp teeth that caged them in.

The Soltan took advantage of the chaos and sprinted as fast as he could for the exit, bare feet clapping against the cool reflective floor. When he looked behind him to see whether the four airborne creatures were coming after him, they'd gone. Relief flooded through him. So why then did his legs feel so shaky and weak?

He looked down and screamed. The flesh had melted off his legs, exposing rotting muscle and bones that cracked apart as mushrooms sprouted through the fractures. The Soltan fell forward, and when he threw his arms out to catch himself, the skeletal hands broke off at the wrists. He could only watch as the rest of his body came apart at the seams, slowly melting into a sizzling goo.

"You can't run," a billion infinitesimally tiny voices said at once, quite matter-of-factly.

The bat swooped down from out of nowhere and clutched what remained of him in its tiny talons. Somehow, it managed to carry him out the window, upward and upward through the smoke and flame, to the highest tower of his castle, and drooped him over the edge of the battlements. He could hear the hungry throngs below, clamoring for him. The air stank of cooking skin and broiling fat.

Before him, the bat's claws transformed into hideous, gnarled hands of leathered skin. There was no longer a bat, just a wizened old woman with long silver hair, eyes as sharp as her nails, a tortured, bloody grimace.

"Now give me a reason," the crone hissed. "Any reason. I dare you, you little shit."

Fergus bolted awake with a birdly screech. He looked around in a mad panic, the distant screams and moans still echoing in his ears. But he was still in the dead forest, nestled up by the side of the road. Quin was leaned up against a tree, watching him, rifle cradled in her lap. *You!* he cried, heart pounding. *What did you do? What did you do? Don't roll your eyes at me, Quin. Explain yourself!*

"Crying out loud," she said in that peculiar accent of hers with its crunchy vowels. "Do we have to do this *every* time you have to stop for your 'beauty rest'? 'Ach, I just had a traumatic nightmare, woman! Tell me what's going on!' Your fault for falling asleep."

Fergus paused. Was that what had happened? Right. Yes. He *had* demanded a brief respite. He must have been more tired than he thought. And he had been dreaming about something. But what, exactly? Something about talking animals. Probably wasn't anything important. Dreams, in his experience, were the brain doing its self-indulgent wankery to exorcise irrelevant and impure thoughts.

How long was I asleep?

"Ten minutes."

You joke.

"No, it was seriously ten minutes."

Really? Huh. Well. I believe I dreamt of talking animals.

"Don't remember asking."

There was a bat. And an owl.

"Huh. Were you at a zoo?"

I can't have been. You weren't there.

"Huh?"

You. Weren't. There.

"I heard you. I don't get the joke. It *is* a joke, right?"

I am implying that you would be a zoo exhibit.

"Ah. That wasn't obvious."

It absolutely was, Fergus snipped. *You're just slow on the uptake.*

"No, you just suck at telling jokes," Quin said as she pushed herself to her feet, brushing some dirt and dried leaves off the back of her trousers.

Growing up, Fergus had been told that witches were old hags with long, pointy noses covered with bursting warts who wore dark sack cloths and pointy hats and went everywhere with broomsticks and wands and maybe some mangy furball familiar. Which was why he didn't believe Quin when they'd first met when she told him she was a witch.

She was somewhere in reach of her mid-twenties and was about average height, with thick red hair mostly done up in a bun and held back with a band, but some of it escaped and tumbled down the right side of her face in a single stream. Her long-sleeved leather jacket was a brighter red, which she wore over a well-filled, wool-knit turtleneck shirt. Her dark, poofy trousers were tucked into knee-high, brown, belted boots.

And of course, there was the gun. Which Fergus was more afraid of as a blunt object than an actual working firearm, as he'd never seen Quin actually shoot it. She sure loved taking it places, though. Perhaps it had sentimental value.

His stomach grumbled. *Quin. I hunger.*

Quin sighed. "Still? You had an entire freaking thing of soup back on the train."

That pitiful cup of sewage couldn't have sated a starving orphan. I need real food. Substance.

"Yeah, well. That was all I could fit into the trip budget. Suck it up until we're out of the woods, Queensworth's just another mile."

The trip budget would have been larger if you would just find another job. Wait, then—

"Then we wouldn't—"

I know, I know, I just—

"BE on the trip, genius."

Fergus sighed. *Thank you, Quin. Seriously though. Have you considered lately finding new employment?*

"I'm not debating this with you again," Quin warned him. "So drop it."

It's an honest question, Quin.

"Yeah, that I'm sick of answering a million times."

It's been nowhere near that many, and I wouldn't need to repeat asking if you would just give me a satisfactory answer.

"Well, why would I want to find another job?" Quin asked, crossing her arms with skepticism over his renewed line of inquiry, leaning herself up against the tree.

Because then we wouldn't have to be out in the middle of nowhere to review what will likely be a terrible show?

"Maybe I *like* reviewing terrible shows," Quin said. "It's *fun.* And it annoys you."

Why? There's only so many ways you can describe how someone's head looks after it's been rendered to pulp by a mallet. Take it from someone who knows.

"You're telling me you don't like the free travel?" Quin said.

Not when it requires this much walking out in the boonies.

"We've only been at this for a few miles."

Which could have been a few miles at a more pleasant locale. Don't tell me you haven't longed for something with a bit more excitement and money in the offing.

Quin pursed her lips in thought. "Weeell, I can always go back to working for Her Majesty."

That perked Fergus up. *Yes! Politics! Now that's where the action—*

"Which would mean I'd have to meet with Esder every day," Quin said, smiling evilly. "You remember Esder, right?"

Fergus swallowed. *Every day?*

"Why do you think I signed up with the *Stardust?* Oh, and did I mention we'd also have to meet foreign dignitaries from various countries you invaded? People from Keniura, people from Lloyer, from Galmone—"

All right, all right. I get it. Well. That's one option off the table then. But we can consider others.

"No, we can't," Quin said as she started back off down the path.

Why not? Fergus asked as he picked himself up and shook himself off.

"Because that's your idea. I don't *do* your ideas. If it's your idea, whatever the opposite is, is probably the safer option."

Fergus cocked his head at her. *So...what if it were my idea to stay an ostrich forever?*

Her back was turned to him, but he sensed she'd just rolled her eyes hard enough to partially loose themselves from their membranous stalks. "God, Fergus. Grow up."

Seriously, though, he said as he caught up with her. *Why do you stay at that rag? I'd have thought after the whole business with the hound derby, you'd have—*

"Be-hup-cause," Quin quickly cut him off while hopping over a short log that had fallen in the middle of the road, "I like writing for money, I'm working with people I respect—present company excepted—and the work's actually important. End of disc..." Quin trailed off and stopped.

What? Fergus said. As he approached, Quin pressed a hand into his feathered chest to halt him in his tracks. Slowly, she turned around to look behind them. At that moment, Fergus noticed the enormous amount of spider webs arrayed in the branches above their heads, woven together to make a thick canopy.

He turned around and looked where Quin was looking, back at the log they'd passed. Upon continued inspection, Fergus realized it was quite human-shaped. It wasn't wood. It was a body, wrapped in thick, slick strands of web. And there was a gaping, fleshy hole in the side.

The two of them made eye contact with each other and looked up. Dangling maybe just twenty feet above their heads, hidden among the branches, was a furry gray spider the size of a carriage, staring down at them with a dozen blue eyes. Its drooling mouth was lined with fangs, and the end of its bulbous body was armed with a pair of barbed stingers.

Quin, Fergus whispered before remembering that he didn't have to. It wasn't like the spider could hear him. *Are you, ah. Going to kill that?*

Quin, staring with wide-eyed horror at the spider, shook her head.

Why? Fergus asked with some urgency.

"Lots of reasons," Quin whispered.

Such as?

"I left most of my magical shit back at the apartment," Quin said.

WHY?

"How was I supposed to know there'd be giant spiders?" she hissed with panicked urgency.

Shoot it then.

"It's unloaded."

Do I have to do every...argh. Quin, listen. There's a talisman in the pouch by my right shoulder. Carefully extract it. But do not cross any of your fingers when you touch it, that could set it off.

While maintaining eye contact with the spider, Quin slowly slipped her hand into the pouch and did a silent double-take when she saw what it was: The Great Seal of the Big Snarg. Who or what Snarg was, Fergus had no clue. The Seal itself was a fist-sized wax talisman whittled to resemble a plump green butt, complete with cheek dimples.

"Um."

Right. On my mark, tell the butt your most dangerous secret and throw it at the spider. Then run for dear life. Dangerous to you, dangerous to someone else, doesn't matter.

Quin's eyes jumped out of her skull. "No fucking chance."

The spider began to lower itself toward them.

Quin, for the love of God, Fergus said, heart pounding. *I don't have to hear it. Just whisper into the buttocks and throw them before we're both turned into spider meal.*

A thick glob of spider drool drooped onto Quin's scalp, rapidly congealing in her hair. Without waiting for another word from him, Quin slowly brought the butt to her mouth and whispered something to it. Fergus was just able to make out the word "folder."

Quin threw the talisman upward. It hit the spider in one eye. The monster screeched and dropped straight at them as the rest of its eyes exploded from the inside out, showering them with hot blue goo.

Run away! Fergus screamed.

Queensworth

Bess stood in her watchtower, weighed down by her mail and bored out of her mind. She could better bear the job of guarding Queensworth's north—and too darn quiet—gate if she just had something to do. Or heck, *shoot*. When the town guard updated from longbows to snapbows, she'd gotten a slick new model with leather grips and yew arms. With a reloading crank! Imported from the capital and everything. They *had* to let her use it. On some tax collector come down from Basdolon, at the very least.

So, the poor little unused snapbow had to sit off to the side in her watchtower, which barely deserved the name. It was more like a treehouse barely ten feet off the ground, and the tree it'd been constructed around was barren of anything, seeing how it was the tail-end of autumn. No birds. No target practice.

Might as well try to chat up Jenny then. Her partner was likewise dressed up in mail and leathers, sword on one hip. She was giving the dead forest down the road a solid squint, nostrils flared like someone had just passed their dirty socks beneath her nose. "Whatcha thinking about, Jen?" Bess asked.

"I'm thinkin' about a fair bit, Bess," said Jenny in her low, earthy tone.

"Yeah? What specifically?"

"Specifically, on some matters of philosophy," Jenny said.

"Yeah? Like what?"

"Well, like on this," Jenny said without looking at her, keeping up her half-squint scowl. "We call this the dead forest, yeah? But nothing lives there. So how can it be considered dead if there's nothing living there to begin with?"

"Um, because all the trees went and died last year?" Bess said.

"They died. Could be. Could be. But what I'm thinking is, there weren't no animals what took up residence before the trees up and died," Jenny noted. "No birds. No squirrels. Nothing. So why weren't it always called the dead forest?"

"Did it have another name before now?"

"Can't recall if it had another name."

"Well...probably wasn't called the dead forest before, I'm guessing, because of the trees."

"What about the trees?"

"Well, trees are alive. I mean, these ones aren't now, but they were before."

"Trees aren't alive," Jenny said.

"Now, you see, Old Man Grinnah, he says they are," Bess said, speaking of the crazy codger who lived up in the decent part of town, and had sacrificed his own ears to try and summon a demon a few years or so back. Funnily enough, losing his hearing had finally forced the old coot to learn how to read. Turned him from the town nut to the town know-it-all, and the founder of Queensworth's pigeon-based mail service. He walked around with some of them sitting on his head sometimes, pigeons. Still something of a nut, really. "Says trees are something called orgasmic, meaning they're kinda sorta living creatures."

"Orgasmic? That so?" Jenny said, her nostrils flaring in a lazy snigger, which was the closest thing she did to laughing. "You'll have to explain to me how that works."

It took her a moment, but Bess realized what she'd just said. Right as her face burst into flame, a patch of forest did likewise. Sparks and bits of forest flew upward, cresting the naked, outstretched tree branches, and a thick black cloud the size of a building mushroomed skyward. The crashing *bang* hit them a second or so later, and behind them, the townsfolk let out a collective shriek of fright and surprise.

"Huh," Jenny said, all stoic-like. With a mechanical motion, she snapped her telescope open and peered through it toward the forest.

Bess did the same, heart pounding. "What *was* that?"

"Was something blowing up, Bess."

"I *know* that, Jenny!" Bess scanned the thick treeline for the source of the rapidly rising column of smoke clawing its way into their beautiful Queensworth sky. "What in hell? What in bloody hell?"

"Could've been our twelve o'clock, maybe?" Jenny said.

Bess looked straight ahead. Two figures emerged from the woods, stumbling. The first was a person, waving a hand about their face like they were trying to ward off a swarm of bees. The second was...Bess had no idea what it was. It looked like some kind of gigantic, long-necked pigeon, except it was covered head to toe in ash. It was shaking violently, trying to get off all the grime, probably. Matter of fact, the person was covered in ash too.

"Ring the bell, you think?" Jenny said.

"Yeah," Bess said. She gripped the bit of gnarly flaxen rope dangling from the big iron bell suspended on a hook outside their little treehouse and rang it three times. That was supposed to declare a reinforcements-worthy emergency and get some help to come around. But a few minutes passed and instead of drawing more guards, it attracted more curious townspeople to the gate. "We need a different bell," Bess said, giving the couple-dozen confused onlookers the stink-eye.

"Why?" Jenny asked.

"So people know they shouldn't be coming toward this one," Bess said.

"I'm not sure I see how a different bell would prevent coming," Jenny said, completely earnest.

"Prevent com…for God's sake, are you doing that on purpose?"

"Doing what?" Jenny said, her lone arched eyebrow straining under the crushing weight of implication.

"Just get your bow ready and look serious. Or more serious," Bess said, digging her foot into her snapbow's stirrup, pulling the string back and loading a barbed quarrel, which she leveled at the ash-covered figure walking toward the gate with the enormous bird.

Said figure turned out to be a woman, hunched with exhaustion and absolutely covered with ash. She was hauling a modest rucksack and carrying a longer, thinner one across her back. As for the bird-thing, it was done up like a pack mule, with all kinds of pouches and other accessories strapped to it that jingled and jangled as it walked. It was pretty much impossible to see exactly what it was carrying, seeing as how the ash had turned everything the same shade of gray. The fact they were a decent distance away didn't help.

"Stop right there, you!" Bess shouted at the woman once she was in earshot, lining up the snapbow's sights with the newcomer's head.

The woman obeyed. And so did the bird, without any prompting. "There a problem, miss?" the ash-covered woman asked in a harsh farmer's accent as she set down the larger rucksack. Almost like her words were trying to claw their way out of the back of her throat.

"You tell us," Bess said, peeved this woman didn't seem to be intimidated at all. She could see the crossbows, couldn't she? "Something just goes and blows up in the dead wood, and the two of you come out covered in ash. We want answers, and we want them now. Make it quick!"

"But you didn't ask any questions, Bess," Jenny reminded her.

"Quit helping," Bess said.

"Oh, the ash, yeah," the woman said as she beat it off her clothes and tried to wring it out of her hairs. "If cleanliness's the issue here, tell you what. You let us in, I promise we'll pay for whatever lodging's got a bath. This one might need a fountain though," she said, shooting a thumb at the bird. The bird jostled its neck, but kept its sidelong glance firmly locked on Bess and Jenny. For some reason, Bess felt faintly judged.

"The ash isn't the issue," Bess called down to her. "It's—"

"Duly noted. Can we come in now?" the woman interrupted.

Bess was very tempted to shoot her. Shoot *someone,* at least. "Is everybody in this city going to give me snark today?" she moaned.

"She's technically not in the city," Jenny said.

"Helping," Bess reminded her. She shouted back down to the strange woman, "No, you can't come in. What do you think of that?"

The woman's face scrunched up in annoyance, which gave Bess a twinge of smug satisfaction. The stranger crossed her arms. "Any reason why?"

"I don't have to answer your questions," Bess said.

"You don't?" Jenny said. "Wasn't aware of that regulation."

"It's not...argh." Bess called down to the stranger, "The explosion, for one thing. If you'd—"

"What *about* the explosion?" the woman challenged.

"If you'd let me finish," Bess snapped. The woman held her hands in the air in mock apology. "Did you have something to do with it?"

"Yes. Fergus caused it," the woman said.

"Who's Fergus?" Bess asked, half-expecting a man to pop out from the tree line.

"He's Fergus," the woman said, patting the bird's back. "He's my pack bird." Fergus the bird's gaze snapped from Bess to the woman with such speed Bess almost thought the bird was offended. "I'm Quin, by the by. Whom do I have the absolute pleasure of speaking to?"

"I'm asking the questions here," Bess snapped at her.

"Yeah, well, so am I," Quin said, with a sleepy half-smirk.

See, this was why there wasn't any justice in the world. Bess had a deadly weapon, and by right, people ought to respect her. But she didn't get any respect, not a drop. "How," Bess said through nearly gritted teeth, "did this...*bird* cause an explosion?"

"Oh. Well, there was this spider—big, I'm talking bloody *big* spider—and being the easily frightened waif I am, I decided appropriate measures were in order," Quin said. "So, kaboom!" She snapped her fingers. "No more spider."

The bird sneezed.

"You said Fergus made the kaboom," Jenny pointed out.

"Don't encourage her," Bess sighed.

"Oh. Well, he pointed out the spider," Quin said with a chortle. "Figure he should get the credit."

"This girl's ribbing us," Bess hissed to Jenny.

"I'd say we're being ribbed, yes," Jenny said. She called down, "How'd you cause the explosion, then?"

"Oh. Well, I'm a witch," Quin said. "I can do stuff like that."

Bess rolled her eyes. A witch. Please. Everyone knew there were only five witches in the whole country, and they all served Her Resplendent Majesty Siobhan the Third. What would one of them be doing so far from the capital? Also, they were all supposed to be really old. Ancient. Quin looked like she was maybe in her early twenties.

"Right, I answered your question. Can you open the gates for us now?" Quin asked. "We've come all the way from Basdolon. We're tired, we're dirty, and we're *dying* to sample your local cuisine." Fergus the bird sneezed, and Bess swore she heard Quin hiss something at him about missing a point.

"What's cuisine?" Jenny asked nobody specific.

"And what exactly's your business in Queensworth?" Bess asked. "Out of curiosity, alright? Me asking you your business don't mean I'm willing to let you in here. Just so we're clear."

"Sure. I've come to do an article," Quin said.

"A what?" Bess said.

"I'm a journalist," Quin said. "From *The Daily Stardust*."

"The what?" Bess said.

Quin's smile wavered. "Uh, *The Daily Stardust*? Daily broadsheet?"

Jenny's eyes narrowed. "Ah, Bess? *Stardust's* got a gun."

"She what?" Bess's eyes narrowed, searching for it...there! Slung across Quin's back. Not another rucksack. A musket. Her mouth fell open. She'd never seen a woman with a gun before. What the hell was she doing with *that*? Did journalists usually carry guns? She supposed it would make sense if they did, considering how they were, by their nature, professional liars. Probably had to defend themselves from people whose honor they'd sullied. "There...there'll be no firearms within the city walls, you hear me!" Bess shouted, eyes transfixed on the gun in mutual curiosity and anxiety. "You need to surrender the weapon once you're inside. I mean, *if* you come inside. No guarantee, just so we're clear."

"Fork my gun over?" Quin asked. The bird made a high-pitched warbling sound. Quin wrinkled her nose at it. "Yeah, all right. Fine." She sighed. "God Alfurious." She pointed at the gate. "Now?"

"Before you fork," Jenny started.

"Not with her, you won't," Bess cut in. "She's filthy. Heh. Right? Right?"

Jenny didn't laugh. "You said you're a journalist," she went on. "Would you happen to have come our way with proof?"

"You mean, like identification? Sure," Quin said, whipping something small out of her pocket.

"What's that?" Bess asked, finger brushing just a few inches above her snapbow's trigger.

"It's my eye-dee card," Quin said.

"Your what?" Bess said.

"Means identification," Jenny said.

"I. Know. What. ID. Means. Jen," Bess lied. She lowered her voice, "But a card? No papers?"

"Doesn't look that way. Definitely odd. Let's humor her for a minute," Jenny said. She knelt down and picked up a large wicker basket the size of a dinner plate, attached to a rope that angled from a pulley. Jenny tossed the basket through their viewing port down to Quin below, slowly lowering it. "If you'd place the card in this basket?"

Quin took a few steps forward, apparently uncaring that Bess still had a bow trained on her head. She took the card and dropped it in the basket, which Jenny pulled up quick-smart and rested on the ledge. The card was an ash-free piece of...Bess wasn't sure how to describe it. It sort of looked like hardened, shiny paper. She'd heard about things like this being popular in the capital.

The card had a colored picture of Quin on the front, impossibly detailed and clear-looking for a drawing. It turned out she was a dark-eyed redhead with pale skin and a small white scar underlining her right eye. The card had a bunch of writing on it. "That Basdolonian?" she whispered to Jenny.

"Don't know. Can't read."

"Yeah, I know, I just…never mind."

"Might be Basdolonian. Looks fancy."

"You think?" Bess had no idea what to make of it. "Well, I still say we don't let her in. We at least gotta get someone out to check what blew up the forest." Bess checked the trees again, and noticed there wasn't any more smoke. "*Without* starting a fire."

Jenny's mouth froze halfway open, staring at something in the basket. "Ah. Bess. Those there before?"

Sitting at the bottom of the wicker dish were two shining gold coins. No, those hadn't been there a moment ago, but gold didn't just appear out of thin air. It was heavy in her hand, sturdy under the pressure of her bite, and had a perfectly pressed picture of the severe, dignified profile of a woman who wore her hair in a perfectly square bun: Queen Siobhan the Second. A real gold piece, two months' wages.

You didn't have to be a genius to recognize a bribe.

The pair of them looked at each other for a moment before Jenny, face flat as a table, pocketed the coin. They stood up and looked back down at the smirking Quin. "We good?" she asked.

Jenny flashed a lightning-quick smirk. "Almost good. You'll have to pay the fee for pack animals."

That wiped the smile off Quin's face real quick. "Oh, come on. Pack animal? Did I say he's my pack animal? My mistake! Fergus is actually my pet." Fergus made a gagging sound that almost convinced Bess he understood everything they were saying.

"City code marks any animal carrying a load as a pack animal," Jenny said. "Whether it's a load of hay or a load of garbage. He's got a bunch of stuff on him, so there's a fee. One bronze coin."

Quin sneered. "Rip-off, load of, son of a..." she muttered as she rifled through a jacket pocket, found a coin and threw it up to them. Jenny caught it out of the air, checked it with a hard bite, then pocketed it. "If you'd please?" Quin said, gesturing to the door.

Thing was, bribes weren't exactly uncommon. Bess had taken a fair few herself. Food didn't buy itself. But the ways this could come back and bite her in the behind lingered in her head. Letting in a woman with a gun? There wasn't enough gold in the world to convince the head watchman to let that go if they got caught.

If. A very big if.

"Well," Bess said, "Jenny and I'll have to take some time to think about whether or not you're a danger. If you could give us maybe an hour or two—"

"Who, her?" Quin said, pointing at Jenny. Her eyes widened. "You say an *hour*?" she wheezed.

Bess smiled. "Yup. Right Jen?"

There was an empty space where her partner had been just a few seconds ago, and an armor-clad woman who looked a lot like her was down at ground level, pulling the gate open with one of the massive iron-wrought handles. "Jen!" Bess cried, feeling herself go red in the face. "I was...you shouldn't be...argh! We're having words over this after dinner!"

Bess snatched her bow and started shimmying down the ladder to give her partner a helping hand. "We'll regret this, I know it," she muttered.

* * *

Slowly, the gate creaked open. So much for an hour or two.

What had been a moderate fragrance until a few seconds ago hit Quin like a fist to the face. Normally, you got the full whiff of towns and cities within a couple miles, but Queensworth had managed to confine the full force of its particular stench behind its walls. Something like horse crap that had spent a few years bathing in vinegar and truffle oil crawled its way up Quin's nose and started scraping at her frontal lobe.

A suddenly blurry Fergus cocked his head at her. *Are you alright?*

With one hand pinching her nose and the other waving in front of her face, Quin tried not to suffocate. "Hagh, fine, hime fi-hine," she wheezed, tears streaming down her cheeks. She waved a hand around for the handle on her pack until she finally grasped it.

After looking back and forth between her and the creaking gate, Fergus sniffed. Instantly, his neck went painfully erect. *Mother of...What is that? What hole have you consigned me to, woman? I've been in torture chambers that weren't anywhere near as pungent as this miasma. It's almost as rank as the Queen!*

Queensworth's gates opened to reveal what could generously be described as a shantytown. Anemic ramshackle homes made from cracked and rotting wood were stacked three stories tall, suffocating each level below. Plank bridges and clotheslines formed spiderwebs between roofs and windows, crossing narrow gaps and alleys. The roads could barely even be called that. There were patches of paved stone here and there, but mostly they were long stretches of thick mud creeping onto wooden porches, sucking on boots and bare feet.

No wonder we never came across anyone coming or going on the way here. This place has all the decrepitude of a leper colony and half the charm.

Quin strode through the gate, trying to look as unbothered as possible with runny eyes. Even though she was covered head to toe in the ash courtesy of Snarg's spider-killing magic butt, people gave her hungry looks. They probably figured if she had the means to get here, she had the money for it too. Pods of haggard children clutched each other from behind windows and in doorways, clinging to each other and watching her with starving, sunken eyes. Their parents and older siblings stood uneasily by, glancing nervously at the pair of town guards.

The black-haired guard with the face like a granite slate—Jenny, the blond one might've said— held out her hand, beckoning. "Your gun, please."

Quin slowly unslung her musket off her shoulder, covertly prying out the small rhinestone embedded into the iron slot on the stock's underside and slipping it into a back pocket. "There you are," she said as she handed the weapon off to Jenny with a forced smile. "Where can I pick it up when I leave?"

"You pick it up at the armory," Jenny said, nodding to a nearby tumbledown shed huddled beneath their watchtower. It was sealed with a padlock and rusty chains that looked like they'd disintegrate with a light breeze.

"Spectacular," Quin muttered.

The blond—Bess—stepped forward, a snapbow resting in her burly arms. Quin's hand shot out and gripped the guard's for a shake. "Quin Schumacher, reporter for *The Daily Stardust*," Quin enthused. "Lovely town you have here."

Bess yanked her surprisingly strong hand away with a yelp. "Idiot! I'm carrying a loaded weapon!"

Quin pouted. "Sorry. Just excited to meet a fellow working woman is all. Say. You still have my ID on you? Gonna need it back."

While Bess started fussily slapping around the pockets of her armor and pants to look for it, Jenny regarded Fergus. "What exactly is he?" she asked.

"Him? He's an ostrich," Quin said.

Jenny looked Fergus up and down with an honest curiosity. "Are ostriches dangerous?" she asked.

"Harmless!" Quin lied.

Curse you, woman, Fergus said, bristling. *At least tell them I'm peaceful. That implies I'm capable of great violence. Which I absolutely am.*

If she hadn't wanted to look crazy in front of dozens of strangers by talking with an apparently ordinary, mute ostrich, Quin would've asked him who he was trying to assure.

"And what's all this he's got on him? They harmless too?" Jenny asked, waving a hand at the copious ash-brushed thingamajigs adorning Fergus. Her finger came dangerously close to brushing against what might have been the Talisman of Urg the Erudite. Which, of course, happened to be Urg's desiccated foreskin.

Fergus stepped back from the guard. *Quin. Please remove this empty-headed covess from my presence before she gets us both killed, and-slash-or she ends up sending the entire block into a pocket dimension.* She wasn't sure if he was kidding, because as far as she knew, none of his gross trinkets were *that* powerful. Fergus checked his other side. *Hang on, no. That's the Amulet of Many Pressed Pants. I think.*

Better safe than sorry. "Um, you mind keeping back from him?" Quin asked. "He's skittish. Still in training." Meanwhile, Bess was still searching every nook and cranny on her person to find Quin's ID. Quin hoped she hadn't lost it, because she wasn't keen on asking Jack for yet another replacement.

A young boy crept out of the shadows, sneaking his way toward Bess, apparently uncaring everyone else within forty feet could see him. If Quin had to guess, he was going to try to pick one of the pouches on her belt. She tried to wave him off. "Not a good idea, ki—"

Quin jumped at the sound of an iron string being violently twanged. "God!" A quarrel planted itself right at the boy's feet. He didn't run away, just looked exhaustedly at the quarrel and slunk off, like he was too hungry and tired to flee for safety.

Quin whirled around and stared daggers at Jenny, who lowered her snapbow. "Just keeping him away from the *harmless* bird," she said.

Quin returned her sarcasm with an equally sardonic smile but didn't take it beyond that. This woman did, after all, have her gun. And a sheathed sword strapped to her belt. Not only that, but Quin couldn't find it in her to be upset at a woman who saw through her bullshit. Intelligence was a charming quality in rare supply.

Bess finally found the card and handed it off to Quin. "Enjoy your stay in Queensworth, Miss

Schumacher," she said, the *hopefully short* clear from her tone. "I warn you." She pointed a finger for maximum warning. "Any trouble, and we'll be on you like flies on food. Got me?"

I hope she didn't hurt herself thinking that one up, Fergus said.

Quin snorted. "Wouldn't dream of it," she said with an exaggerated grin. She pocketed the ID in the same jacket pouch where her two recovered gold coins—swiftly palmed off these ladies with a little misdirection and a dab of magic—rested. She gave them a two-fingered salute and walked off, checking behind her a couple times to make sure they weren't about to be called back. Or they weren't being tailed by overeager townsfolk.

Once they'd rounded a quiet corner, Quin took a breath, her heart racing. "Phew," she said. "Glad we weren't searched this time. Or shot."

Bah! They should've searched us. You, at the very least. The incompetence. The blatant lack of skepticism and proper procedure. Truly disgraceful. I'll bet it'll take the rest of the day for them to notice you robbed them. You did *nick those coins back, right?*

"No, I let them keep them because I was feeling generous."

Hmph. You know, back when I still held my station as Death Lord, I made sure to institute a stringent policy to ensure all of our constables were of the finest caliber and integrity. I started by—

"Ferg," Quin said, "If the punchline includes the words 'removing' and 'women'—again—I'll hex you so hard you won't be able to tell where it itches, but by god will it itch. Fucking *bad*. In somewhere you'll never reach."

Fergus sniffed. *If I can't reach the itch, wouldn't that help me narrow down where it would be?*

Quin gave him a look. The kind she reserved for catcallers and street preachers.

Well goodness, message received. He surveyed their surroundings, which weren't much different from the gate, except now the ramshackles went up to four stories. *And the local government can afford to maintain a legitimate combat arena? Quin, trust me on this. If you find any pamphlets talking about liberty and equality, we need to get out of here before the quarrels start flying and the riffraff starts barricading all the roads with parlor furniture.*

"Ferg, you're really lucky I'm the only asshole who can hear you. Revolutionaries would single you out for the chopping block in two seconds flat." Quin batted at her clothes a few more times to get the rest of the ash off. "What do you say we do with a wash?"

You read my mind, Fergus said without an ounce of irony. *We'll of course need the absolute finest of accommodations. Which, considering the locale, might mean a small tent behind an outhouse.* He nodded his head toward a more crowded avenue. *Come. I am an unequaled inn-spotter.*

"Good reason to keep you around."

Among many others, I'm sure.

He started off, and Quin was about to follow him when something hiding down the adjoining alley caught her eye. Two kids watched her from beneath a tent made of sackcloth and a big stick, mounted atop piles of trash. Quin tore her eyes away from them, felt guilty, and looked back. They were still staring.

Quin tapped a finger behind her ear. The children remained motionless, though their eyes registered a faint twinge of confusion. She repeated the gesture.

One of the kids got the hint, stuck his fingers behind his ear, and jolted. Out came something gold and shiny. Thankfully, he had enough sense to immediately hide it in the rags barely clinging to his filthy body. The other kid plucked a coin out of her ear and squealed in excitement. Quin pressed a finger to her chapped lips and winked.

Right as she caught up with the sexist bellend of a bird, whose inn budget had just gone down two shiny pegs, something caught Quin's eye: a few drooping strands of her hair gone silver. She gasped.

What? Fergus said.

"Nothing," Quin said as she twirled the hairs around her finger and yanked them out, throwing them away. Fergus grunted, but thankfully didn't press it.

Quin breathed a sigh of relief and made a mental note to tone down the magic.

Plight of the Gladiator

When Quin was asked to do a review of Queensworth's gladiator pit and its upcoming three matches, stretched out over the course of several days, the first thing she thought was, "Aw, shit." Queensworth was the kind of name for a city with no redeeming qualities, where the local city council wanted to trick suckers into swinging by because maybe Her Royal Majesty had popped in for tea and biscuits at some point. Worthy of a Queen! It was like a business including the name of its home country or the word "patriot" in its newspaper ads.

Which was why when Fergus led them to a squat, deteriorating brickwork building with cracked windows called *Royal Hospitality,* Quin shriveled.

Here, Fergus said, stomping into the mud for no other apparent reason than for emphasis, hard enough to launch flecks into Quin's face. She flinched, scraping the new grime off her chin and forehead with spiteful care. *We'll lodge here.*

"No," Quin said.

Yes.

"No," Quin insisted.

What, you would rather keep looking?

"Maybe."

Well, Fergus said, *this looks like the sort of place so desperate for travelers they'd book an ostrich a room. So, I'm willing to settle.* He sniffed. *And whatever they're cooking in there, it smells expensive. For here, I mean. I shall partake.* Before Quin could stop him, Fergus walked through the open doorway. A scream erupted from inside.

Quin rolled her eyes and trailed after him.

Four silvers were enough to rent Quin a space for herself for the next two days—and to keep the terrified tavern-keep quiet—because there was no chance in hell she was staying in Queensworth any longer. When she asked for a room specifically for Fergus, the frightened innkeeper nearly swallowed his tongue. All things considered; it was a mild reaction compared to what Fergus shouted at her when she arranged for him to room with priests who were passing through town. Cheaper that way, and she'd take any opportunity to spend a night away from him and his disgusting toys. But she had to give Fergus credit: It was impressive how angry he could sound without using curse words.

After he was led away to his own accommodations, Quin went upstairs to her room and locked the door behind her with the provided key. There was a small dining table, a corner bathtub half-hidden behind a folded wooden screen, a twin bed with feather pillows and—eugh—*paisley* quilts. There was water-rot in the holey ceiling and the floorboards were dusty with termite shavings. And there was mold somewhere, she could smell it. Though, better this than a back-alley tent.

After setting the pack with her extra clothes in it down, Quin went to the window with the spider-web cracks, pulled it up and peeked outside. The place had a view of a dark and smelly alleyway, filled with offal and what might have been a dead body. She ducked back in and slammed the window shut before she got flashbacks of her witch training.

I would like to state for the record I do not appreciate my current predicament.

She started at the sound of Fergus's voice. Great. He was doing this again, even after she'd told him already to stop. Fucking. Doing it. It creeped her out when he talked to her through walls, and she had no idea how to block his voice.

Making him telepathic in the first place had been like knitting a gown out of stinging nettle while blindfolded. Somehow, she'd done it, and it was too big of a hassle to try and figure out how to undo it.

Thankfully, as far as she knew, that was the extent of their little mind-link. Fergus couldn't read her own thoughts—she'd made sure the first week they'd been saddled together. First, she'd imagined him fucking his own mother—Quin had seen pictures of her. Fergus hadn't reacted. Then she imagined a plot by herself and her so-called sisters to sacrifice Fergus in a dark ritual to completely raze Jocrom. Again, nothing.

But even then, she hadn't been *completely* sure. So, she'd envisioned some magical cube-thing that, when touched, would restore him to human form, and it was under her bed back at their apartment. The quarter-inch thick layer of dust beneath her queen-size was, to this day, undisturbed. Though it did leave the somewhat unnerving possibility he *could* read her thoughts, was savvy enough not to give it away, and was planning some kind of long con to take elaborate revenge on her.

Still, the mistake of making him telepathic didn't come close to how boneheaded it had been to clue him in she could hear him through walls. She only wished she could talk back and tell him where to stick it, without having to shout.

The fathers have taken to discussing amongst themselves how best to cook me, Fergus went on. *We may need to escape into the night, Quin. I can't guarantee I will be able to restrain myself much longer against these bald, proselytizing freaks. I don't suppose you might be willing to restore some of my powers to me so I may resurrect and show off whatever's making that stink behind the drywall? Would give the fathers quite the shock, I'm sure.*

Quin yawned.

Come on. Imagine their caterwauling!

Quin stretched and let out a lengthy fart.

Very well. Interestingly enough though, they don't seem to mind me taking a bath. Though I had to keep tapping the nozzle to get one of them to run it without revealing the profound extent of my intelligence. It's a tricky balance, bathing without getting any of my items wet. Thankfully, none of my items of power are reactive to water. So far as I'm aware. I suppose I should have asked you to remove my things beforehand, but as your heart is black as coal, I suspect you would have declined to offer assistance.

Anyhow, I assume you'll likewise be bathing soon, sans in the view of men of the cloth, so I will go silent for a while. Dinner's on you.

Quin didn't want to think about dinner right now. She just wanted to get bloody clean. Bath time. Two firm twists to the tap made the pipe tremble and vomit out rust-red water. "Oh, lovely," she muttered, letting the stuff run until it eventually came out clear. Once the tub filled up, she stuck a finger into the water. It was frigid. "Bloody fantastic."

She stripped and lowered herself—chattering like a nervous dental patient—into the icy water, scrubbed her skin raw and wrung her hair clean at lightning speed, then jumped out of the bath, shivering violently. Too late, she realized there were no towels. She dried herself with one of the bed quilts, dropped it to the floor, and put some new clothes on from her pack. Fresh undies and socks, plain shirt, wool turtleneck sweater, black trousers. Even with all that and her jacket, she was still cold, so she wrapped herself in the last remaining quilt.

Once she was warm, she shed the blanket, cricked everything needing cracking, stretched, and decided to get the ball rolling on her article. Off to the Crescent, then. She took a small gem out of a pocket hidden in her jacket's inseams.

It looked like an ordinary child's marble, except for the single dot of light at its center burning with such brilliant intensity it cast a single shining beam across the whole length of the room.

Her last chiroptera metamorpher. Using it would allow her to arrive at the Crescent in short order, let her get the lay of the land. She could scout out the rest of the city, and maybe even sneak into the Crescent if it was guarded. And she could use it for a hasty escape, if needed. If Ben Medina was really being held captive somewhere inside the Crescent, the metamorpher would almost guarantee she'd find him.

Plus, it would cut down on the walking—never a bad thing.

But did she really want to use it? Each one cost a fortune, plus the soul of a necromancer. And harvestable necromancers weren't exactly easy finds anymore.

Over in his room, Fergus began to sing, tunelessly and without much in the way of rhythm:

Oh, I knew a barmaid from Latar,
Verdant and tall was she,

She'd jump around that cold dark bar,
And show her grapes for all to see!
Purple were they, red was her face,
Plucked from the vine was she,
But instead of milk that came from those...those...drat, is there a synonym for breast that rhymes with face? Chaste? No, that's its own word, that'd be stretching it...
Meh. She secreted wine for all to see! Ho!

One harvestable necromancer.

Trying her best to ignore Fergus's godawful drinking ditty, Quin tossed the marble into her mouth and swallowed. Once she felt it go down her throat, she snapped her fingers. She felt the gem break in two as it plopped down into her stomach, releasing its pow—

Her heart leapt into her throat when she realized she'd forgotten to open the window. She bolted for it as a feeling like her bladder was rapidly filling began to spread. Into her organs, her bones. "Oh shit oh shit oh shit oh shit shiiiit!"

She pried her fingers under the frame and threw it open so hard the glass shattered. There was a sound like a bundle of sticks being snapped in half, and Quin was a bat, flapping her leathery wings in the middle of her shoddy hotel room. With a relieved squeak, she flew out the open window into the cooling evening air.

Quin wasn't huge on being a bat, if she were being perfectly honest. She'd never liked having a sudden, overpowering craving for locusts. The last time she'd given into that temptation, she'd had bug guts on her tongue for a tortuously long bridal shower.

She wasn't great at flying either. Five stories skyward was all she could muster before getting light-headed, but even two was enough to get a decent view of the rest of Queensworth. It was a nasty little pimple of a town, swollen and threatening to burst some vile gunk out from its depths. A latticework of dilapidated woodwork slums with the occasional patch of brick.

It didn't take Quin long to figure out which building was the Crescent—it looked like one. A moon-shaped-and-colored stone colosseum in the dead center of town, with a curving slope of tiered bleachers making their way down to a sandy pit that edged up against a sheer ten-foot drop into a wide river bisecting the town—butter-soft ripples of bloodied twilight shimmering across its surface. Smart move, building the colosseum along the river. You could wait until the limbs had been collected, then shove in the unusable, unsightly bits for whatever mutant river-creatures could survive somewhere like Queensworth. Crocodiles with nine legs or some such.

Quin carefully descended toward the arena, checking for any possible guards or transients who might be living around the place who might see her. Colosscums were popular spots for the homeless, and why not? If you could sneak in, they were relatively safe so long as your fellow bums weren't considering robbing you in your sleep.

She capped off her descent at about ten feet above the highest rung of bleachers and spotted a small group of haggard custodians sweeping the stony floors and scrubbing the benches with buckets and sponges. While they didn't look dangerous, Quin didn't intend on popping back into human form in front of them.

Ben Medina would probably be beneath the colosseum itself, in a hypogeum. She landed in front of the iron grating closing the arena off from a dark and foreboding corridor. She scuttled her way through a gap in the gate's bars and took flight again.

One of the biggest benefits of being a bat was having excellent eyesight for the dark, and this helped Quin navigate the otherwise unlit corridors leading into an armory with an orange glow bleeding through the gap separating it from a straw-strewn floor. There were no open portholes or other gaps for her to move through. Back to human form, then.

Quin landed and looked for somewhere she could store the rest of the metamorpher's remaining power and still swallow without having to make a painful trip to the toilet later. There: a small pebble. She touched it with her little bat claw and let the magic flow into it. As the tiny rock began to glow and flash, Quin got taller. Less batty.

Human again, she dropped the pebble into one of the front pouches on her jacket and pulled the door halfway open, hesitated for fear of possible guards, and grabbed at a rack for the nearest weapon: a nasty-looking, serrated...huh. A breadknife. Gripping the handle tight, she slowly creaked the door open and peeked through.

Beyond was a simple jail with a curved ceiling, torches resting in sconces hammered into the brickwork. Each cell was about ten by twelve feet, equipped with a bucket and straw pad, and what few occupants were awake shied away from Quin as she passed them. To her surprise, most of them were thin and poorly dressed. They kept to the corners of their cells, shivering or eating scraps from wooden bowls. These definitely didn't look like gladiators.

Except for the man five cells down, a slab of muscle half-hidden in shadow who had to be seven feet tall. He reclined against the wall of his cell, one arm resting atop a raised knee. He stared at her as she walked by, yawned, and bowed his bulbous head to rest.

Now, it wasn't necessarily illegal to use prisoners or criminals as game fodder—assuming that's what some of these people were—but this was many more unfortunates and strings of gristle than Quin had ever seen in one place. And that definitely struck her as odd.

She did two passes up and down the cages, but she didn't pick out Ben Medina among the dozens held captive. "Ben?" she tried. "Ben Medina?"

Quin flinched as she heard a thumping sound behind her. A woman lying on her cot away from Quin lowered her hand from the patch of wall she'd just been pounding and thumbed leftward. Brow furrowed, Quin checked the next cell, where a man laid sideways on his bed. She leaned back to the woman's cell. "He know where Ben is?" The woman gave a thumbs-up.

Quin set the bread knife down, picked up a bit of grit off the floor and flicked it at the man's bare shoulder. "Hey," she whispered. "I'm looking for a Ben Medina. Is he here? Is he still—"

The man bolted upright from his pad and twisted around. He was as brawny as he was hairy, and his nose looked like someone had taken it to more than a few grindstones. Quin wouldn't have been surprised if a cat had used the rest of his face as a scratching post either. His head had been recently shaved, and his topaz-colored eyes were sunken in their sockets, but they sparkled with excitement. He hobbled off the straw, dragging a peg leg crudely harnessed to his left knee, and practically threw himself at the bars. Tears of relief raced through the carved grooves in his hollowed cheeks.

Quin took a reflexive step back, but when she looked closer, she saw traces of the meek politician she'd interviewed several years ago. She still had to check. "Ben?" she whispered.

He nodded eagerly with an excited grin revealing several missing teeth. What few were left were broken. A couple looked like they'd been filed down to fangs.

"I got your note. I..." It probably wouldn't have been a good idea to bring up the fact his couriers had tried to jump her and Fergus and had died for their trouble. Just in case they'd been his friends, and not some escapees who'd been doing him a favor. Hopefully, he wouldn't ask after them. "Never mind. You remember me?"

He shook his head.

"Quin Schumacher, *Daily Stardust*. I interviewed you for—"

Ben slapped a hand to his forehead and gestured at her as if to say, "Now I remember!" He nodded.

"There a reason you're not talking?" she asked him.

He opened his mouth. His tongue was gone.

"Eeegh. They can't do that with *everyone* around here. Do they?"

A few nods.

"They do?"

One nod.

"The hell." A colosseum with gladiators who couldn't sling insults at each other? Since the review was still in the cards, the Crescent was going to find itself on the receiving end of a merciless lashing, courtesy of Quin Schumacher.

She crept in close. "Listen. The Witch of Basdolon. You were talking about Esder, right?"

His expression hardened into a spiteful grimace. Another solemn nod.

A mix of excitement and dread swirled in Quin's chest. On the one hand, it was confirmation, the starting gunshot to let her story take off. But the nagging moral obligation to put the story out would place her right in Esder's path.

Esder. Personal secretary to Queen Siobhan the Third. The Flayer of Lloyer. Exploder of faces. Getting on her bad side was, to put it mildly, the end-all-be-all of dumbfuck moves.

Then a vision of a large two-bedroom apartment flashed in front of Quin's eyes, with a living room relatively free of ostrich feathers, and her hesitation evaporated. She took out her pad and pencil and handed them to Ben through the bars. "I need you to put that down in the record, all right? Tell me what happened. You don't have to use whole words."

His eyes shone as he scribbled something with a renewed energy. He checked it, scrutinized for the angle catching the most torchlight, then showed her what he'd written:

Free me.

Quin grimaced. "Yeah, ah, not sure I can manage that, Ben. Sorry."

Medina's face fell. He wrote something new below it:

You're a witch.

He was appealing to her powers, not insulting her. And questioning why she wasn't using them to bust him out. Or maybe he was accusing her of being in on it somehow? She guessed she couldn't blame him there, she was Esder's "sister" after all.

Speaking of: How did the others factor into this? Quin swallowed. What if Johanna or Avery knew about this, or were a part of it? Lorena, she wouldn't dare, she was too much of a bleeding-heart goody-two-shoes to consider doing so much as jaywalk. But all of them had been contracted not to get involved in politics, just to do what the Queen asked of them. About non-political things. If that could be circumvented somehow, then so much of what she knew about how things worked among the Five would have to be horseshit.

She shook her head, grounding herself back in the here and now. The others couldn't be involved. They just couldn't. They were about as fond as Esder as she was. And besides. If they were involved, she would have noticed. Probably.

Quin went on the assumption that Ben was appealing to her powers and said, "I'm aware. But there's only so much I can do with my magic without...you know, let's not get into it. Point is, I didn't come here to free you, Ben. I came here to get your story out there on paper. And if I help you out of here, then I can't do so."

Confusion flashed across his face, followed by anger and disappointment that crescendoed into a crushing hopelessness. **I fight him tomorrow. You MUST free me.** He pointed past her to the seven-footer resting in the cell across. Quin grimaced. Medina definitely wouldn't last long against that big bastard, but what was she supposed to do? Even if she did want to help him—and she did, just a little—she had absolutely zero experience with breaking someone out of a prison, and she couldn't imagine getting her feet wet in that department with a man who only had one to speak of.

If they were pursued, they'd get caught. Either by Queensworth's own authorities, or much, much much *much* worse—Basdolon's. From there, it would only be a matter of time before word got back to the Court of Repentance. Then Her Majesty. Then Esder.

Quin shook her head. "I'm sorry, Ben. I can't. And from an ethics standpoint, I can't tell people what's happening here if I go and stick myself in the middle of your jailbreak."

Medina slumped like a puppet whose strings had been cut, collapsing against the bars of his cell, his back to her. Then he set her notepad down and pushed it to her.

"Ben, come on. I know this isn't what you're hoping for, but..." She trailed off as she considered what he *had* been hoping for. An eleventh-hour rescue to keep the Crescent's floor from being painted with his brains. Shit. Quin crouched and picked the notepad up, slapping it against the other palm as she tried to think of something comforting she could say. Maybe there was something she could do, but what? She doubted the local constables would do anything, and she wouldn't trust Fergus to save anyone's skin but his own. Any other promises she could make would be platitudes.

Except maybe...

"Hey. You like revenge?"

Medina shifted.

"Thought so. Who doesn't, right? You spill your guts to me, and I'll...oh, ah, sorry. Forget I said that. Ahem. Meant to say, you tell me everything, and I promise you I'll see Esder's skinny ass on a spit by the end of the month. You know how many people read the *Stardust,* Ben? A whole bloody lot, that's how many. You've seen issues at Congress Hall, right? The stands in the lobby? We're practically everywhere. I guarantee you, by the time Esder knows what's happening, she'll be straight fucked. Everyone'll know what she's done. And there'll be nothing short of burning Basdolon to the ground she'll be able to do about it. Which Siobhan would never let her do."

Medina pushed himself off the bars and reoriented himself to face her. He nodded at her in a way that seemed to ask, "Do you mean it?"

Quin nodded. "I really am sorry I can't do more, Ben. But whether you or not you realize it, this is more important than you. Esder shouldn't have done this. God only knows what it means for the state of the government." She proffered the pad to him. "So, I need you to write down your testimony. People need to know. About you. About all of it. And hey, a little bit of retribution on the side never hurts, right?"

He gave a resolute nod and started scribbling at an energetic pace. **Sent here months ago. Sham trial for espionage. Others too.**

"Others? Like, other charges?"

He shook his head and pointed at the opposite cages.

Quin's eyes widened. "Other *people?*" Well, shit. The scope just ballooned. Hell, maybe people would actually give a shit. It was one thing if a forgotten politician with no family had gotten himself thrown to the wolves. If Esder had disappeared someone people actually cared about, that'd be pretty much impossible for her to bury.

He nodded, beckoned for her to give back the pad. **Two other civil servants I know of. Coworkers.**

"Was that Esder too? I mean, she sent them here?"

I think so. Don't know why.

"Who? Who were they?"

Catherine Bockrath and Nelson Deveraux.

Whoever they were. Quin foresaw research in her future. "They still alive?"

No. He started writing something else, then faltered and frowned. He crossed something out. ~~But maybe they~~ **Wouldn't Esder be a conflict of interest to you?**

Quin winced. Right. She hadn't considered that. Why hadn't she considered that? She racked her brain to find some way around the problem but couldn't think of anything. Did it really matter, in the long run? As much as the thought made her squirm, she might have to let objectivity take a backseat to the truth. So, she'd have to be sneaky about how she got this article to print, because Jack turned down news pitches the moment he caught the faintest whiff of some kind of bias.

"Maybe," she said. "But I'll work around it." She nodded to the notepad. "Keep going. Write down as much as you can."

She sat with Medina for the next hour, watching him write, occasionally starting at the sound of a distant door being opened or shut, but no guards ever showed up. By the time Medina was done, almost two-thirds of her notepad was filled with frantic scribblings in plain handwriting. He was about to hand it back to her when he thought of something else, jotted it in a corner, then handed the pad back. **Written in the hand of Benjamin Medina, former Minister of Foreign Communications for Her Majesty's government. Year 3831, High Autumn, day sixty-two.**

"Thank you, Ben," Quin said, stuffing the notepad into the front pocket of her jacket. Ben gave her a thumbs-up and a weak attempt at a smile, but the welling in his eyes betrayed his terror. No wonder, it wasn't like this was going to save him from being smashed to a pulp tomorrow.

Her stomach sank as she realized she was going to have to watch. After all, she still had a review to write. Though maybe, just maybe, she could use that to her advantage here.

She stood up and pointed to the door. "I guess I'll be going."

Medina grunted as he rose to his own feet. Well, foot and bit of wood. He gave her the Basdolonian salute: hand splayed parallel to the ground, thumb jabbed into sternum, then folding the hand so it covered his heart.

Quin gave him a thumbs-up and left, taking a torch on her way out to better navigate back the way she'd come. She wasn't giving him that salute. Nobody she liked ever gave that salute. And she didn't want to chance those teary eyes of his changing her mind about rescuing him.

When she was back at the main hypogeum gate, she tossed the torch behind her shoulder, downed the rock, turned back into a bat, crept through a gap, and took to the skies. Outside, the evening light had given way to night, a light dusting of stars sparkling above. As Quin ascended, she felt a tug at the back of her tiny gullet. Damn. She'd used up more of the metamorpher than she'd thought. She had maybe a minute's worth of flight left, nowhere near enough time to make it back to the *Royal Hospitality,* and she wasn't risking transforming anywhere above six feet.

Quin found a quiet stretch of street and turned back to human form. "Whew." Now she just had to wait until midday the next day for the actual match. Which brought back the ever-present question: What the hell was she going to do until then?

Once Quin became a witch and opened herself to the Five Streams, she'd stopped sleeping. Didn't need to anymore. She missed having good dreams. Mostly because the sandman had sometimes blessed her with the chance to relive beating the living shit out of her father.

But if she ever found herself pining for a trip through dreams, she'd remind herself of her nightmares. Well, nightmare, really. The same one she'd had since she was little: A sky painted in the color of smoked flesh; air crushed by the stench of accelerating rot. A walled city burning to the ground. People on fire. People *eating* each other.

And the screams. God. The screams.

The dream always came in such sharp relief the details seemed almost amplified. It was constant, relentless. Then it had come true: She'd been seeing the night Harashin, capital of Jocrom, fell. When she'd met Fergus. When she'd seen him turn his powers on the city's entire population in a desperate attempt to defend himself from Quin, Johanna, Esder and her personal goon-squad of Sunspots.

Quin warded the memory off with a shudder. She had no idea how or why she'd been dreaming about that for so long before she became a witch. She'd never asked the others about it, for fear of what they'd do to her.

"Quit thinking about it," she chided herself. She'd figure out how to kill time back at the relative safety of the inn. Besides, it would be a good idea to familiarize herself with the route from here to there, seeing how she'd come back tomorrow morning anyway, with Fergus in tow. And if he really wanted to go through with his insane plan to conquer Queensworth and use it as a base of operations to launch his comeback takeover of the kingdom, who was she to stand in the way of his getting killed? So long as he didn't put Ben in harm's way somehow. Wait, right. Ben was already buggered. Damn.

A half-hour walk later—which had quickly gone from a nice, casual nighttime stroll to a constant game of checking over her shoulder to making sure the shadowed figures a dozen strides behind weren't actually following her—she made her way back to the inn, went upstairs to her room and found a shriveled banana peel, black as the night, impaled on her door with an enormous hunting knife.

Quin leaned in for a closer look. Nope, not a banana peel. The foreskin of Urg the Erudite, the one Fergus was half-sure had extraordinary destructive powers. "Well, if that's not a threat," she said as she jimmied the knife out of the door and flicked the dried willie off down the hall.

Knife aloft, she gently twisted the knob, kicked the door open and burst into the room, now brisk from the chill coming in from the window she'd destroyed. Nobody lying in wait she could see. Quin checked all the corners and crannies, half-expecting Fergus to pop out from somewhere and declare his prank. Either that or try to kick her for his own amusement.

But there was nobody home, and her belongings didn't look like they'd been rummaged through. There was, however, a note laid out across her bedspread, inked in plain Basdolonian script. She carefully stabbed it through the middle with the blade, in case the parchment was poisoned. Quin turned her back toward the window so she could read the note in the moonlight.

"Red Woman," she read aloud. Hm. Not a bad title, if a little generic. "We have your bird. Come to the corner of Weatherby and Birch at midnight with five gold coins, or you shall never see him again." It wasn't signed, but she could tell from its tingly, vaguely foul aura that it'd been written by the priests Fergus had been rooming with.

Quin lowered the letter. She kicked the door shut, stabbed the blade into the tiny dining table, threw herself onto her bed—big mistake, the mattress was like a damned rock—and grinned to herself through the discomfort. "Free at fucking last!"

For a moment, she pondered the potential danger of letting Fergus's various talismans and other objects of power wind up in the wrong hands. She decided that was very much *his* problem.

Quin groaned as she sat up, back throbbing. She took out her notepad and began brainstorming how to disguise an exposé of political assassination by way of involuntary gladiatorhood as a colosseum review. However she did it, it couldn't be her usual style. Fergus had said something earlier in the day about adding flavor. Not a bad idea. About damn time he was useful to her in some way or another.

She'd make it raw. Gritty. Easier to get to the truth of everything.

But first things first. Quin began reading through Ben's account.

A Fresh Alliance

You craven child-diddlers! Fergus bellowed as they hauled him, bound by the feet, from the cart and carried him toward the recently-arrived iron cage—a prisoner wagon. They'd taken him to some lonely, misty street corner and waited around for Quin for what had to have been hours, and if he had to hear one more insipid word from his kidnappers about the difference between Incolf weather and Keniura weather, he was going to try his damndest to swallow his own tongue. *I know where you're sleeping for the night! Once I am free, I shall extract mighty and terrible vengeance upon you! I'll cut off your manhoods and force you to cook them into an ironic vegetable stew, then feed them to the hogs for slop!*

Of course, they couldn't hear him, thanks to that scarlet harridan who'd cursed him, curse her. *Quin,* Fergus said none too calmly as they heaved him. *If by any chance you're within a reasonable distance of my person, I hope you realize you're letting the Death Lord of Jocrom fall into the hands of...* A trio of bandage-wrapped men emerged from the other cart, and the priests handed Fergus off. *...Whoever these smelly, poverty-stricken lepers are. Unhand me, you filthy—ACK!*

The bandaged men tossed him into the cage and slammed the back hatch shut with a quick click-clack of a lock. *Ow.* After squirming around, Fergus managed to adjust himself into a more comfortable position. At least there was straw he could cushion his head on. *Quin? Aaaaany time now.*

Reins were snapped, and they were off. The poorly paved roads bounced the cart around like a shuttlecock being prepped for a good whack. He struggled in vain against the ropes binding his feet. Alas! If he only had his powers, he could have resurrected some local street rats—of either the two- or four-legged variety—and get them to climb into the cart and chew away his ropes. But bound up and powerless as he was, all Fergus could do was make pathetic mewling noises.

He wondered what they were going to do with him. Probably eat him, if the two priests' conversation from a few hours ago had been anything to go by. It'd been considerably foolish to turn his back to them, giving them the opportunity to stun and wrestle him to the floor. The result had been considerably awkward, since he'd been wet and naked. Then again, he was usually naked.

Perhaps he'd be sold to some local butcher who wanted a break from cutting up his neighbors and unlucky stray dogs, or whatever else peasants ate. Maybe they intended to eat him alive or use his member for some kind of dark occult ritual. After all, the penis had innate magical potential. It was arguably the most flexible of all body parts, in the magical sense. You could burn it for a sacrifice, call forth a demon through calculated shagging, or eat it to temporarily gain the powers of its owner...Fergus swallowed at the thought of priests possessing the power of a Death Lord. Musket ball dodged, he guessed.

More often than was probably warranted, he wondered whether turning him into a bird known for its monstrously large beef cutlass—that he couldn't capitalize on—had been a deliberate consideration on Quin's part. He hoped not, because that would be a masterstroke of calculated cruelty worth saluting.

Everything went dark as the cart hopped into a pitch-black tunnel. At this point, he had no doubt the crimson strumpet wasn't going to come swooping in to rescue him. Fine then! He would do perfectly well on his own. He was Fergushar the Tenth, Democratic Emperor and Death Lord of Jocrom, Soltan of the Pale Star, whose powers had no equal, even as an ostrich. Whatever bind he found himself in, he'd be able to break himself out of it. Rope notwithstanding.

The cage screeched to a stop in some sort of dark enclosure, with a few sconce-trapped torches casting meagre light, just enough to illuminate sets of iron bars beyond his own. Was he in some kind of prison?

"Here we are, lovely," said the rough, yet oddly melodic baritone of the driver. Fergus caught a hint of mockery, and wondered whether he was the addressee, or someone else. "Your steed for tomorrow, as promised! Told it's something called...an emu, I think? The two of you'll surely make a better show for tomorrow than the cripple."

Fergus choked. *An emu? An* emu*? You syphilitic, dirty-nailed, pig-fornicating swain! I am an ostrich. An ostrich! I'm no long-lashed fairy princess!* Then he caught the operative word: *Hang on, steed?* Steed*? What're you on about?* He twisted his head. Past an iron gate, there was a small, impressively pale woman with short dark hair, wearing leather armor desperately in need of repair. She stared at him with exhausted eyes. Eyes with black "whites," red irises and gray pupils.

A vampire. Well. You didn't see those often.

Fergus hissed as they opened up his cage and took him by the feet. *You barbarian! Have some respYOW!* His head caught what had to be a splinter as they dragged him to the floor. One of the lepers unlocked the door to the vampire's cell and started dragging Fergus to her.

Fergus inhaled. He didn't really need to, but it was habit: *QUIN! HEEEEELP! I'M GOING TO BE EATEN!*

The vampire hissed and clapped her hands over her ears.

Fergus gasped. *Did you just...*

They plopped him into the dank, cold-floored cell and walked out. Creak, slam! Imprisoned. Wheels scraped across dirt, then trundled away, slowly fading out.

The vampire stood above him with a quizzical look. *I warn you,* Fergus said, trying to sound braver than he felt. *I probably taste like whore-witch magic and dead people.*

The vampire's eyes practically popped out of her head. She craned an ear toward the fading click-clacking of the departing cart's wheels, and once it was completely out of earshot, pointed a finger at him. She formed a mouth—or maybe his head—with her hand and mimed talking.

Fergus took in the look of shock in her eyes. Did he dare to hope? *You* did *hear me, didn't you?*

She nodded excitedly.

Oh! He composed himself as his excitement swelled. *Oh. Well. Hm.* Fergus wasn't sure whether to be elated. On the one hand, he'd been starving for conversation with someone, *anyone* who wasn't Quin. On the other, he was in a cell with a vampire. Did vampires feed on ostriches? He had to learn more about her, at least. Figure out whether he was in any danger, and regardless of the answer, find a way to use this to his advantage. *Are you deaf?*

She shook her head.

Mute, then.

Nod.

Well, can you write in Basdolonian script?

She nodded again, a little more enthusiastically. Fergus looked toward a patch of brick-laid wall, dimly lit with torchlight. He shook himself to check whether he still had any of his talismans on him that he wasn't lying on. Just a pouch or two of jingling trinkets, but otherwise, they'd stripped him bare. Of course. He cursed the priests for robbing him of the Nose of Airborne Calligraphy. He could have used that about now. *Is there something you can write with? Perhaps you could break off one of those nice pointy teeth of yours? I'm sure they grow back, do they not?*

She opened her mouth. All her teeth had been removed. As had her tongue.

Ah. Well. I hope you kept the receipt from the dentist. At least now he was confident she wasn't about to eat him, though her lack of fangs did raise the question of how she'd been surviving up until now. He imagined it was probably very difficult to draw blood without teeth. Perhaps they'd been serving it to her. He conjured an image of this woman draped across her inhospitable floor, gently swirling a wineglass filled with a dark, viscous liquid.

Anyhow, you'll need to find something you can write with. By the by, where are we anyway?

The vampire made a crescent shape with her hands.

Fergus swallowed. *Ah.* So that was what the bandaged man had meant by a show. Then he was to die on the morrow. Splendid. But at least Quin wouldn't be able to write about it. Her precious journalistic *ethics* wouldn't permit it.

Then the leper's words came back to him. *Forgive me, but did that man said you were to...ride me?*

The vampire grinned and nodded. She mimed holding up a pair of reins, skipped around in a small circle like she was galloping, then waved a hand down her face like she was shutting a visor.

Oh no. Oh *no.* They were going to use him for jousting. *Good God. Where on this miserable continent am I? What kind of sick, twisted establishment jousts using ostriches? Are there more ostriches? Are all the jockeys...jousters, whatever they're called, are they vampires too?*

After a sustained bout of charades, he got his answers: The Crescent—little smart-aleck—shrug, no, and no.

I see. Regardless, he needed to plot his freedom, and fast. Fergus had no intention of perishing in front of a cheering crowd. *Listen friend. I may not look it, but I'm a necromancer of great power.*

The vampire guffawed.

No, truly! I admit, I don't look like much. I was cursed into this form by an evil witch who forced me to serve as her pack mule. It's an awful, dramatic tale, I assure you. But believe me when I say I'm a mighty force to be reckoned with. All you need to do is protect me when we're out on the field of battle, and once we have a tidy collection of corpses, I will be able to raise an army of loyal zombies. Trust me, those snowball pretty quickly. Liberation and power will be ours!

So what do you say? Allies?

The vampire pensively stroked her chin, considering. *Oh, come now, woman. What do I need to do to convince you?*

She retreated into a dark corner of the room and came back dangling something between her pinched fingers. A dead rat. She pointed at it and raised her eyebrows.

Fergus tried to hide a swallow. It occurred to him it probably hadn't been a good idea to toot his own horn over his necromantic abilities when he hadn't successfully used them since he'd been human. But one could hope. Especially when facing down a bloodsucker, defanged as she was. *A rat? Oh yes, I can manage a whole rat, it should be—*

The dead rat rotated just enough to reveal the enormous ribcage-exposing wound in its other side. Not so whole.

...A breeze. Well. Such was life. As short as his was about to be. *Put him down in front of me, would you?*

She obeyed. Fergus examined his assignment. Maybe it would work this time. After all, up until now, he'd only tried bringing humans back to life. Small animals had been a cinch back in the day.

Now. Bear with me here, but I need you to retrieve my Dead People Baton. It's just along a fold of skin along my back. Yes, along there, a bit to the side, keep reaching, warmer, warmer, cooler, warmer, red hot! Fantastic! Now, if you'd insert it into my open maw?

The vampire obeyed, and Fergus warbled the Song of Resurrection aloud while waving the baton. After decades of corpse-reviving, he had the routine down pat. But trying to force the tune through his birdy vocal organs was another beast in and of itself, especially with the baton in his—

The rat twitched.

Fergus stopped singing and gaped, quickly clamping his beak shut again when the baton nearly fell out. No. Could it be? Hope and elation exploded inside him as he resumed the song, "singing" with as much passion and volume as he could muster without releasing the baton again. The rat's one visible eye opened, revealing a pale-purple orb swirling with necromantic power.

I did it! Fergus squealed as the rat rose to its feet, shook itself off, and shot off into the inky dark. He could barely believe it. After years of trying in vain, only to be slapped around the beak with disappointment time and time again, it worked. For the first time since his empire had fallen and he'd been cursed into this putrid form, he'd brought a body back to the world of the living. Tethered a little slip of soul back to the fleshy meat-sack that had once housed it. Raised a stiff, by God!

It worked! It really worked! How? Why? Did it matter? His powers had returned!

The vampire clapped for him with a thrilled grin.

Haha! Does that prove my worth to you, madam?

She nodded, but held up one finger as if to say *wait.*

What? Fergus said.

She mimed what appeared to be a cutting something in half. Then a scale equaling out. And a sideways letter V, formed with two fingers.

It took Fergus longer than he'd care to admit figuring out what she was getting at. *Ah! Equals. You want to share power. Is that it? You want to rule together once we've conquered Queensworth.*

She gave him a thumbs-up.

But of course! In her pint-sized dreams. *I would be happy to provide you with half of my forces as payment for helping me survive the trials to come. You shall have the finest zombie gladiators seen this side of Incolf. I would draw up a contract or provide you with a limb to shake, but seeing as how you still haven't freed me from my bonds, that's a little difficult.*

She hooked a finger into the ropes and gave them a gentle tug. They snapped away, and Fergus was finally able to right himself and put his baton away. *Ah! Much better.* He took in more of his surroundings. There were numerous cages outside, and in the one opposite of theirs, there was a thin young man practicing punches. He couldn't have weighed more than a hundred pounds and looked like he'd fall over from a light nudge.

Maybe not the *finest* zombie gladiators, but enough. Fergus considered his new cohort. *Ah, one last thing. Would you mind writing your name on the wall for me? I would like to know with whom I have the pleasure of wreaking glorious havoc.*

The vampire took off her belt and used the buckle to scratch a name in Basdolonian script on the wall, which he was just barely able to make out.

Hm. Now that I think about it, couldn't you have done that earlier? You know, it doesn't matter. Good to meet you, Brand. I'm Fergus. Now, let's talk tactics as best we can.

Blood, Babes and Boners

Headline: Politics Get Down to Bloody Business in Queensworth
Subhead: Former Basdolon Civil Servant Goes Out in Crescent Opening Bout

By about eleven in the severely overcast morning, the crowd is already out for blood. You can smell it, even over the warning scent of oncoming rain from the dreary black clouds. Everyone's all jumped up, hyped up on violence, snorting it up like crushed spice. There's wire-tension in the air that's waiting to snap from just the slightest flick of your finger. If you close your eyes outside in the square, it almost feels like you're in there already. People shouting and screaming, kids shrieking, air all hot and stuffy.
The Crescent draws you in, even though it curves toward the river. You stand there in the square with its back turned on you, like you're in bed with a lover who's turning down sex just to spite you, and their curving, clean back makes it all the worse (change this later). Say what you will about Queensworth, at least they know how to whitewash a wall.

To get in, you gotta go through this narrow door built into a thick iron gate filling up this archway like a spider web in someone's mouth. The bouncer's a thick fellow with a mallet crusted over with people-bits. The ticket taker right by him's a scruffy-looking kid (fix that contraction) with a tacky burlap uniform with fake bloodstains, like he'd just crawled out of the ring himself. It would have taken a crowbar and a miracle of G-d to pry his eyeballs off my chest.

"Ticket?" he asked me.

"Yeah, one." I gave it to him. "Who's today's match?"

"Mm? Yeah. Flaming Nip and the Single-Leg Slammer."

"They any good?"

"I dunno," he whines. "What're you doing with your fingers?"

"Playing my imaginary piano."

He gives me my ticket back after punching a hole in it.

As far as seating goes, the Crescent's no Entrailion. The seats are hard stone with absolutely no cushioning to be found. You've got maybe enough room for your feet so they don't break off at the ankles from being bent for two hours, and if you can go an entire minute without getting a gob of spit in your hair, you've got the Devil's own luck.

The Crescent may be a shitpit, but it's got atmosphere. It can hold two thousand or so people, and by the time it's filled, you're sandwiched between two wild crazies shrieking themselves bloody and the local urchins are raking the arena floor for the tiniest scraps. Some spotted-pate geezer auctions off his aisle seat to two burly beer-bellies, and the loser starts beating the living piss outta the other.

The Crescent's trademark snack is an overpriced fried rat on a stick. It's seasoned with cayenne and rosemary and tastes like a rat seasoned with cayenne and rosemary. So like chicken, but shite. Shite, not shit. Important distinction.

Two rats later and a woman in thin, flowy skirts emerged from one of the big iron gates connected to the underground hypogeum. Everyone cheered, either because this meant blood was finally about to be spilled, or because her breasts were one hop shy of popping out of a black-painted whalebone corset. The lusty, crooning wail bursting from the whole damn arena when she traced her fingers over them settled that little debate.

I had a sinking suspicion that nobody had ever accused the Crescent of being subtle.

She plunged her hooked nails into the spots where each funbag met collarbone and flung out eight fanning trails of scarlet flecks. There was a sound like a cannon going off and the red spray snapped into a burst of flame. The crowd screeched itself raw, irreversibly hoarse.

"Who's she?" I asked the round, crusty-bearded slob sitting next to me.

He looked at me like I'd just said the weather was controlled by a secret cabal of child-eating groundhogs. "She makes me rigid!" he said.

Well. How about that.

She started dancing, doing lots of little twirls and flips in time to a faint drumbeat. She added a little pyromantic stripper flavor to it, setting herself on fire and burning away little bits of cloth off her body, until all that was left was the corset. I hadn't heard cheering and screeching that loud and enthusiastic since my mother's execution.

Then the woman exploded. Suppose when you've gone that far, you've gotta commit to the bit. The crowd was one deafening, horny scream. Like a legion of wheedling, randy tomcats. Though there wasn't any gory spray, which disappointed the couple dozen

attendees sitting in the splash zone.
A ten-foot-high column of flame
erupted from where she'd been
standing and split in two. The
whirling flames gradually pulled
away from each other, and with a
twist and a lick, they vanished and
left two sets of proud warriors
behind.

On the left was a hulking man with
bigger badongas than the opening act,
replete with swirly tattoos
emphasizing his fat brown nips. Said
nips were shooting fire out of them
like a dragon with hiccups, which
distracted just a little from the
terrifying, mean-looking cleaver
this hulk of muscle and fat was
hefting around in his meaty paws. The
only part of him armored—and clothed—
was his crotch area. The Flaming Nip
had to be somewhere around seven feet
tall.

Across from

Quin's link to her typewriter in her apartment in Basdolon fizzled and died when she finally noticed who the Flaming Nip was going up against: eight full feet of definitely *not* Ben Medina. Her jaw was halfway to her feet by the time she jumped to them. "Fergus, you motherfucker!" she screamed at him, only to be drowned out by a din of cheers, whoops and peals of braying laughter from the bloodthirsty crowd. Down in the pit, Fergus had been saddled— where in the hell did they find an ostrich-sized saddle?—to accommodate a tiny woman who couldn't have been more than five feet tall. She wore tattered leather armor and wielded a long, thin rapier, which she flipped and flicked around by both the handle *and* the blade, teasing more appreciative whoops from the audience.

Fergus, other than the tiny saddle, was wearing some milk-white parody of the kinds of drapes and skirts you usually see on a jousting horse, from his minute skull down to his lean legs. He looked like a drugged-up artist's vision of an abstract lamp, and if she had to guess, the white was to make it easier to see the blood. Under any other circumstances, she might've taken a few guilty licks of pleasure from seeing him look so ridiculous. As it stood, she was finding it painfully difficult to resist the urge to hurl herself down there and rip him apart.

She heard his voice, faint but recognizable: *Quin, I know you're amongst this blood-crazed throng, so all I have to say is this: Good luck writing your way around this one, you horsewhipping, harlotting hack! Yow!* He cried out as the woman kicked his wings and spurred him into battle. *Look at me! I'm a conflict of interest! In a dress!*

"*Ooh,* I hope that fatass crushes your skull, you misogynistic, bird-brained, elongated chicken-looking scumfuck!" Quin howled as she reached two hundred miles away to eject her now-useless story from her typewriter and hurl the handful of pages to the floor. "Harlotting's not even a *word!*" She sat back down, smoldering, crossing her arms and her fingers in support of the Flaming Nip.

Bastard. Bastard *bastard.*

Though she couldn't deny, there was something weirdly majestic but still deeply infuriating about the sight of an ostrich used to lording over an entire country being ridden into battle against a half-naked gladiator with swirly, flame-belching man-boobs.

She didn't *really* want Fergus to be down there. Even without the capacity to speak, someday he'd get himself killed, that was practically a given. Couldn't keep his opinions to himself, couldn't resist using forbidden magic, couldn't erase the fact there were people out there who would have loved nothing more to revenge themselves upon him for all the horrors he'd inflicted. He could at least have gotten himself disemboweled without ruining her story.

But now he was down there—about to die and looking disappointingly excited for it—circling around the Flaming Nip, bobbing and weaving his ridiculous neck away from angry, frustratingly slow swings. The Flaming Nip bellowed and roared, his wrathful glare firmly glued to the grinning woman affixed to Fergus's rump, who'd tossed her helmet away. She had no teeth.

"Eugh."

As the fight dragged on, Quin managed to force some calming breaths. There were another two days to go. Two more fights, so it was still possible Ben would—

The woman was suddenly airborne, flying at the Flaming Nip's face like she'd been launched from a catapult. Her toothless maw yawned open and an entire second jaw popped out, lined with shark-like teeth, all serrated and pointy as spears.

Quin felt the blood drain from her face as she recognized just what Fergus had been saddled with. "Oh fuck."

The Xalic vampire tore a fist-sized chunk out of the Flaming Nip's throat, sending a gory spray into the crowd. Wine-red blood bubbled out from the enormous gladiator, and none of his fat fingers were able to stem the flow from the meaty ruin blooming beneath his chin. He fell flat on his back with a dull thud. Fergus trotted happily about the corpse, drinking in the crowd's adulation as the vampire did likewise from the gladiator in greedy gulps.

Quin squirmed. Not so much at the sight itself, but because one of the handful of creatures that genuinely terrified her sisters was practically within spitting distance.

She forced herself to relax. The vampire didn't know she was there. Also, Fergus didn't know where she was, and knowing him, he probably had zero idea what a Xalic vampire could even do. So as long as Quin didn't give herself away, she'd be...

Fergus went over to the body and drooped his head toward it.

Quin swallowed. It was fine.

He retrieved his baton and started waving it around like a child playing soldier. She couldn't hear him make his usual warbling.

It was *fine*. He'd never been able to use necromancy before, why would today be any...

The Flaming Nip's body was twitching. Quin was back on her feet. "No." It was FINE. They were just death-spasms, there's no way Fergus's powers would come back *now,* of all—

She looked at the Xalic vampire. She was staring down at Fergus, and her wide eyes were a deep pitch-red. Amplifying. Empowering. A cold nausea swept over Quin.

The Flaming Nip's sightless, vacant eyes turned a deep violet.

"Fergus! Fergus you bloody moron, no! NO!" Quin screamed.

The crowd cheered even louder as the Flaming Nip sat back up. They didn't seem to find at it all concerning when his head slowly swiveled around to stare at them with glowing, pulsating purple eyes.

Quin made a beeline for the exit, shoving aside any man, woman, and child who was stupid enough to be in her way.

* * *

Victory! Fergus roared, baton held high. He scanned among the crowd for Quin and spied her racing for the exit. *Yes, run! Run away, Quin! Spread word far and wide, for you have borne witness to the return of the...* He caught himself just in time. Brand could hear him, but could she hear him when he was talking to Quin? Could Quin hear him when he was talking to Brand? Either way, in case his newfound vampiric compatriot didn't share his political leanings toward full fascism-by-zombie, he could gloat without announcing his full title. At least until he'd disposed of Brand. You never knew, this enormous lard with the odd chest tattoos was large enough, and she small. Maybe he could get him to eat her.

The gladiator—what was his name again? His real one. Brand had told him...hmmm...ah! Luscious, that was it. Odd name. Now he was a big, walking slab of meat who could punch people really really hard and create more zombies for Fergus to control.

Wait a moment. Would a zombie obey telepathic commands? Was necromancy compatible with witch-crafted telepathy? Hm. Well, there was no time like the present for an experiment. *Luscious!* Fergus showed him the baton. *Be a gentleman and tuck this away in the usual place, would you?*

The gladiator obeyed, gently inserting it into the feather-concealed fold of skin along Fergus's back.

Splendid. Now! Go down into the dungeon and kill as many other gladiators as possible.

Luscious lumbered down into the hypogeum, earning many boos from the crowd. Another success! Fergus happily strutted around the perimeter of the arena a few times, Brand walking alongside him and waving her blade at the crowd. *Yes, more! More! I revel in your loathing, filthy peasants! Gnash your few remaining teeth at your new master, for it shall be your final opportunity!*

Once the rotten fruits and snacks started sailing toward him, Fergus decided to keep a healthy distance from the crowd.

Screams and snapping bones echoed from the dark depths of the hypogeum. Fergus winced. *Careful in there, you lummox! I...we need them intact. Well, relatively intact.*

There was a pause. Then he could hear the distinctive *thud* of skulls being slammed against brick and stone. Fergus sighed as well as an ostrich could sigh.

The booing dwindled and surrendered to a mix of cheers and gasps of shock as the other zombies lumbered out in messy file. They dragged their entrails and broken limbs, leaving trails of blood and viscera behind them. *Ah, my army of the dead. Welcome.* Fergus snapped to attention. *Inspection! Line up so I can get a good look at your splendid flesh.*

Men and women in various states of dress and armoring formed a clumsy line. Fergus couldn't help but feel a little short-changed on account of their poor quality, and he'd had the whole night to eyeball these sorry sods. But at least they'd been whole, then. Now, every single one of them was an absolute mess of pulp and bone. Luscious, evidently, hadn't been delicate. Brand vaulted off his back and approached them, staring slack-jawed—likely as disappointed as he was—at one man with a peg-leg and most of his skull caved in. It was hard telling whether the pink mass oozing out from behind his broken teeth was tongue or brain.

Still, most of them carried knives, cleavers, maces, axes, swords, clubs. They would do, all two-dozen of them. Just enough to get the avalanche started, and they looked functional enough. The crowd certainly seemed to appreciate their appearance, though Fergus figured that was because they'd erroneously surmised the games were about to resume and the undead before them were, in fact, in elaborate costumes. Bloodthirsty dullards.

Right then. All of you, go into town and cause some havoc. Nothing too destructive, mind. A broken window here, a city block burned down there. Just enough so we earn the Queen's ear. We need her to send over a few locomotives-worth of platoons to recruit into our ranks. That was the beautiful thing about the Fergushar family necromancy: it spread like the plague. Once a zombie killed another healthy mammalian meatsack, another zombie earned its membership into the undead cadre. Aah, the convenience and ease of conquest. Intoxicating as taking a whiff from a full bottle of a flowery port.

Luscious the zombie gladiator was the first to depart. He clumsily vaulted into the stands, caught a foot on the railing and fell flat on his face hard enough to snap his head back and break his neck. That earned some scattered, appreciative whoops from the crowd. If Fergus had hands, he would have slapped one to his face.

The crowd didn't seem to appreciate or quite expect it when Luscious—face now angled skyward—got back on his feet and started breaking peoples' necks.

And neither did Fergus, beak hanging open in shock. *What...what are you doing, you imbecile? We have to subjugate the peasantry, not recruit them!*

Then the other zombies climbed into the crowd and started hacking, slashing, and clubbing their way through the screaming masses. Mowing down the living like they were wheat. A child's head rolled down the stairway and bounced into the arena, landing right next to Fergus's feet. It looked up at him with dull surprise.

That...was a little much, he had to admit. *All of you, back down here, now! We'll be having more than a few words about what it means to have a sense of discipline!*

The zombies continued their massacre, painting the stands red with the blood of the hundreds who were already crushing their friends and family to death in their vain attempt to flee for the exits.

Stop! Stop, you empty-headed nincompoops! Your master commands you, by the power of Fergushar the Tenth! Democratic Emperor and Death Lord of Jocrom, Soltan of...

They weren't listening to him. He swallowed with growing concern.

Brand, he said. *We might have an issue.*

Brand slowly turned to face him. She pulled an enormous hunting knife from her bodice and gave him a humorless, toothless grin. He found himself uncomfortably reminded of his mother. She'd used to give him a similar smile right before she went to her chambers to retrieve the paddle. The one with the tiny spikes on it. His backside prickled.

Uh. Brand. I'm not sure I like the look you're—

He screamed as she let out an unholy war-shriek and launched herself at his face, knife slashing.

Shouting and Standing About

"Fuck fuck fuck fuck fuck fuck fuck fuck fuck fuck!" Quin wheezed as she bolted from the Crescent, down Queensworth's muddy, boot-sucking streets, darting around people and shoving the stubborn ones out of the way. She shouldn't have used that metamorpher, should've saved it for an emergency like this. She should've known Fergus would go and pull some fucking stunt. She just hadn't expected him it would be as stupid as to partner with a Xalic vampire. Any magician worth spit knew they could amplify and siphon other people's magic.

So now there was a tiny, newly minted vampire overlord cavorting somewhere in Queensworth without any direct sunlight to kill her and a spreading zombie army under her control. All thanks to Fergus. If she survived this, she'd make sure he wouldn't, damn the Queen's decree.

First things first. She needed her gun.

By the time she reached the gate she came through the day before, Quin's lungs were a pair of rusty bellows, and she took gulps of rancid air like a fish that managed to swim its way up a filthy toilet and beach itself on the seat. "Hagh!" she wheezed, waving her hand up at the sad little watchtower. "Hagh! Ha-ha-heeagh!"

The two guards, whatever their names were, peeked their heads out over the top of the wooden barrier that was supposed to protect them from god only knew what. Bored children armed with rocks, maybe. "Oi!" barked the more expressive one. "You're the woman from yesterday. The ashy one."

"She does appear to be the woman from yesterday, Bess," said the scowling one.

"I know Jenny, I just said." Bess threw Quin a hard scowl. "Those...offerings you left us. They up and disappeared. Mind telling how you went about that before I get angry?"

"Zah, zagh," Quin managed to choke out. She didn't consider herself all that sedentary a person, but her breathing did make her wonder whether being a septuagenarian in a twenty-year-old's body could really be considered healthy. She jabbed a furious finger in the direction of the Crescent.

"You saying there's trouble? Down that way?" Bess said.

"I would say it's a safe bet she's indeed saying there is trouble down toward the Crescent," said Jenny. "Is that what you're saying, Miss Schumacher?"

"Yes...for...love of...fuck," Quin wheezed.

"Come on, Jenny," said Bess. The two of them slid down a ladder and jogged to Quin, crossbows slung across their banks. "What's your issue?" Bess asked Quin.

"What exact trouble are you trying to tell us about?" Jenny asked.

Quin gulped down one long breath and managed to force more words out. "Get...ugh, me...hagh...my...gagh...gun." With every word, she stabbed a finger at the padlocked shack they'd pointed out to her yesterday.

"Your gun? Why do you need your gun? What're you going on..." Bess trailed off as a series of screams pierced the air. They came from the direction of the

Crescent, and several plumes of smoke had started up too. "...About?"

"What's happening over there?" Jenny asked.

Quin took a gulp of air. "There are...agh...a bunch of gladiator zombies tearing through town. They're being controlled by a tiny vampire, and the only way to kill them is to either...hagh...either to cut off their heads or kill, kill the vampire. She's immune, com*plete*ly, to all conventional weaponry, and the weather's not going to be of any hel—"

A fat drop of water smacked Quin in the back of the head. She grimaced. Shit. Of all the rotten luck. She'd hoped that the sun would burn off the cloud-cover, then the vampire. "Yeah. Bottom-line, the only thing within fifty miles that can kill her is locked up in the glorified backhouse you've got standing there."

Bess let out a disbelieving half-laugh, but when she saw Jenny's hardened expression, she went silent.

"So before some upright cadaver comes and tries to take a chunk out of one of us, please." Quin pointed to the shed again. "Get me my fucking musket."

* * *

Fergus blinked his left eye open. He was on the ground, lying on his side and his skull felt like somebody had stuck it into a vice. *Oh. Ohhhhoho.* If a hangover could make vicious love to a migraine and produce spawn, this was the result. The random droplets of rain crashing into his face didn't help.

He tried to recall what happened...right. Brand. Hurtling toward him with a freakishly huge knife.

Him blacking out when she buried it in his neck and starting sawing. *And I'm not dead. Odd.* Another wave of pain plunged its fingers into the folds in his brain and began kneading. *Ohhh. I wish I were.*

He peered upward. *Huh.*

The recently packed Crescent now hosted a scant bunch of idling zombies. Some gave him empty stares from their seats, waiting for a match that was never coming, bloody drool dripping out of their open mouths and torn-open throats. The misting rain was sluggishly washing the copious amount of blood down from the bleachers into the fighting pit.

Screams and cries drifted in from outside the arena, loud and sharply pitched. Panic and confusion and desperation, all perfectly composed into a nostalgic, zombie-conducted oratorio. *Well, things seem to be moving along as planned,* he said.

He tried to move, but all he could do was jerk his throbbing head. That was concerning. He also couldn't feel anything below his considerable neck. That was also concerning. Was he paralyzed?

A shadow fell over him, a looming, ominous shape. Fergus swallowed, hesitant to face it. What would be worse at this point for him to find looming? Brand? Quin? God? The apparitions of his parents? He looked up.

Somehow, the reality was both a relief and profoundly worse. It was a headless mound in a white dress stained red around the neck's stump, attached to two spindly pink legs that were, at this moment, doing the can-can.

Oh God. That was certainly a sight no man should ever have to see. His independent lower half sauntered off, still dancing.

Fergus distracted himself from the sight by checking for whatever bodily functions remained available to him. All his physical and mental faculties from the neck up seemed to still be in working order, but he couldn't breathe. And he didn't need to. Odd. Why?

Perhaps my magic has some kind of self-preserving aspect I'm not aware of? Fergus asked the lone zombie within earshot. Pretending he had a conversation partner was surprisingly relaxing. *Bah, no, that's ridiculous. Death Lord of Jocrom I may be, but I'm fairly confident my necromantic abilities don't stray far outside the ordinary. I've certainly never heard of a necromancer getting offed and continuing to endure through their own magic.*

Also, I'm absolutely conscious. Zombies are not. At least, you're not in the same way as live humans are. I've done experiments on it, as a matter of fact. Wrote a paper and won an award from the Board of Black Magicks at the University of Zhai Ezan. He chortled. *Then I had those geezers all catapulted into the Purple Sea. Patronizing, blatant backside-kissing twerps, all of them. I plagiarized that paper to the pit and back, and they knew it. Not sure why I did that though, in hindsight. The plagiarizing, I mean. I did* do *all the experiments.*

I digress. Point being, you can't form thoughts, recall memories, anything of the sort. And I'm doing all of that, without any strain. Of course, if Quin were here, she'd probably say something like, 'Are you sure, Ferg? No effort at all?'

Hmph. So, what could this be? Maybe...

Fergus had to roll his eyes at himself when he finally managed to reach the conclusion he should've arrived at several minutes ago. *The scarlet strumpet's magic, of course. Well, isn't that just absolutely splendid. Now I owe her twice over for...God's sake, would you stop that?* he barked to his still-dancing body. *You're not making either of us look particularly dignified, you know. And you're being distracting.*

His body turned to face him, and leaned slightly askew, as if to cock the head it now lacked.

Don't tell me. You can hear me too? Raise a leg if you can. His body raised one leg. *Splendid! Though it seems like whatever limits Quin placed upon me are...conspicuously arbitrary. To say nothing of currently conversing with myself, despite you not having ears or a brain.*

Putting that aside, time is of the essence. Find Quin and lead her back to me. She'll need me if we're to revenge ourselves upon Brand. Now go!

His body did what might have been a bow, then shot off straight into and bounced off a wall. It landed on its side and started kicking, hard and fast enough to gain some degree of traction and make circles in the muddied ground. It looked a little like a dying beetle trying to right itself.

Fergus sighed. *Well. I suppose I shouldn't have gotten my hopes up.* He watched his body spin around, and found himself oddly transfixed by the long, slender legs as they gracefully kicked in defiance of the weeping heavens. *Bah! Curse her. They* are *fabulous.*

* * *

Like its four siblings, Quin's rifle had been fashioned out of flowing black wood stripped from a tree in the darkest pit of Hell. It used the bone of a demon for flint, the sands of Paradise for powder, and the rest of its metal components were made from dragonfire-heated steel strong enough to withstand getting run over by a beaching steamer. The stock had a slot for a protective crystal that kept its already-powerful wielder from getting disintegrated by the magical recoil.

With these guns, Quin's sisters had brought entire kingdoms to their knees. Killed gods. Penetrated the veil between reality and the unknown. Show-offs.

"Um," Quin said, holding the thing in her hands like it was some halibut she'd just caught on her first fishing trip. She looked up at Bess and Jenny, cheeks flushing. "Would either of you happen to know how to...ah...load one of these?"

Jenny gave her an unimpressed frown. "You don't know? It's *your* firearm."

"Yeah, well, I haven't used it in bloody forever." Forever being more along the line of four decades. Ever since, it had been more of a point of pride and a symbol than a working, lethal weapon. As well as the occasional improvised jacket rack.

"Did you see any other muskets in there, lady?" Bess said. "We barely have the budget for bow upkeep. Never seen one before until yours."

"Well, great," Quin said as she examined it like it was her first time laying hands on it. And for all she'd used it, it might as well have been. When she noticed both women were watching her, she pointed in the direction of the chaos. "Don't wait up on me, there's a gang of walking dead roaming through town. You helped me find my gun. Thank you. Now leave me be and go help."

"Oh no, we're not just about to go and let you waltz around town with a firearm," Bess said.

"Really, *that's* what you're worried about?" Quin snapped.

"Especially," Bess said with a defiant pout, "if you don't even know how to use it. Come to think of it, why even go around with a gun if you don't know how to use it? Where's the responsibility in that, hm?"

"Lecture me about responsibility again, I'll turn you into a frog without back legs," Quin seethed at her as she fumbled around the unloaded gun, trying to remember whether she was supposed to load a shot by dropping a ball down the barrel or sticking it in some kind of port.

"Oh, come off it, you're no witch," Bess said. "Witches don't need guns, besides."

"Well, thank god for that, looks like I'm pulling out my own hair for nothing here," Quin said as she snapped her fingers right under Bess's nose and made a silver coin appear in her pinched fingers. Bess gaped.

"Huh," said Jenny with all the enthusiasm of someone pretending to be impressed by their date putting away an entire steak in less than a minute.

Right as Bess reached for the money, Quin stuffed it into her jacket's front pocket, where she rooted around before plucking out the purple protective rhinestone and loading it into the slot built into the gun's stock, twisting it clockwise once. *That* at least she remembered how to do.

She bet Fergus knew how to load a musket. No point in asking him about it, seeing as how he was probably carting that vampire around the place, raising the dead left and right.

The gun needed musket balls, that much she knew. Thankfully, she had a little tin of spares. Except she'd left them all with…

Quin slapped a hand to her forehead and dragged it down her grimacing face. "Aw, *no*." Once she came to terms with what she'd have to do, she snapped her fingers at the two watchwomen, reclaiming their attention as they began to bicker with each other about whether they were authorized to kill zombified townsfolk.

Bess scowled, though she did have the sense to look more wary of Quin now. "We're not dogs, you know."

"I gotta go find Fergus."

"Who?" said Bess.

"Her bird, remember?" Jenny said.

"He's got my musket balls," Quin said.

"Yeah? Well, that's nice," Bess said. She held her hand out to Quin. "Just give us the gun and you'll be off."

"Why? We just let her have it," Jenny said.

"Because—"

Quin shook the gun in Bess's face before she could get another word off. "Look at this. This here? It's the only thing that can kill the vampire with an entire bloody zombie army, which, by the way, is currently between us and Fergus. The *only* thing, got it? Nothing else'll do the job. And any other magic I use within fifty feet's just going to make her stronger.

"If I can't separate him from her and get my ammo? If I can't fix this omnishambolic catastrophe and word gets out the town's a living fuckpit of undead? Her Majesty'll send the Sunspots out here to take care of it."

"Sunwhats?" Jenny said.

"Sunspots. You both know what palefire is?" Quin asked.

Bess and Jenny tensed up and gave her nervous nods.

"You ever seen a pyromancer work with the stuff? That's a Sunspot. And they'll start launching that shit over the walls without a single damn given for anyone inside."

Bess's mouth worked soundlessly. After a few seconds, she stopped trying. "Um, Jenny?" she whispered, whiter than bone. "Maybe we should…"

"Absolutely," Jenny said, steely faced but equally pale.

Bess swallowed. "Right. Then let's go find…your bird's name is Fergus, you said?"

"Aye," Quin said, slinging the gun's strap over her shoulder. She looked the two up and down. They both looked like they were shitting themselves, but they weren't running. In fact, they had a steely determination in their eyes. Bravery, raw and genuine.

"Well, if you're coming, c'mon then." Grimacing to brace herself against the oncoming fresh pain and acidic taste that came with burning lungs, she ran back toward the Crescent.

* * *

Now, just a couple degrees to the right. Watch your footing, watch it! Good. Good. Now, just a bit, one foot a time, watch the pebbleaaare you kidding me! Fergus shouted as his body hopped around on one foot thanks to the offending pebble, before losing its balance and falling on its side again. *You're useless, you hear me? Useless! What do you have to say for yourself?*

His body just kicked at the air helplessly.

Fergus sighed inwardly. What was it? What had he done to deserve this absolute abject humiliation, watching his body flop around like a fish left to die on the splintery surface of some stinky pier? What terrible inconveniences could he have possibly committed against Jocrom to warrant this finite existence as a decapitated bird head, watching his unsightly bird body kick a circle into the blood-spattered coliseum dirt like a child denied sweets?

He was being silly. Of course he hadn't done anything to deserve this. Hadn't he been a benevolent, kind despot? He'd only purged when there wasn't enough food to go around, tortured to put quick ends to uprisings, and catapulted the elderly into the ocean when his citizens needed a good laugh to keep their spirits up. Hardly extraordinary, as far as atrocities went.

But ruminating on how unfair life was wasn't going to get him out of this predicament. He had to escape this arena and find Quin, get her to put him back together. If she could. He really, *really* hoped she could. *Alright, let's try this again. Up! Right yourself.*

His body flopped onto its back, kicked at the air a few times, then hurled itself upright, planted its feet and pushed itself into a standing position.

Good! Good. Now, come to me. His body began walking in a straight line, perpendicular to him. *No, no! Stop. Rotate...approximately ninety degrees. I'll tell you when to stop. That's good, good...stop! Now, come toward me. Slowly, slowly now! Careful! You step on my head, we're both...I'm...whatever. Stop!*

His body stood above him, waiting.

Finally, he'd gotten it over here. It only took him what felt like a hundred tries. Fergus wanted to sigh in relief, but, well. No lungs and all. *Good. Very good. Now. Kneel.* God, how he'd missed saying that. It was more than a little surreal, saying it to himself.

His body knelt.

Lower. He'd missed saying that too.

His body obeyed.

Loweeeer, Fergus cooed.

His body knelt so low he was now eye-level with his own open trachea. Blood and what might have been saliva trickled out of his throat-hole.

Eugh. Too low, but that should work. So! Now comes the tricky part.

Much Ado About Various Assorted Anatomies

Quin kept a decent jog for about twelve seconds before she devolved back into a wheezing, choking mess, so she wound up walking with Bess and Jenny into the oncoming field of zombies. Well, not really a field. More of a sparse, poorly tended grove, easy to maneuver their way through. That was the thing about zombies: So long as you kept out of arm's reach, you were fine. They just flailed about, like barstool drunks failing to reach the tantalizing top shelf.

Or so she'd been told. A vice-like grip snatched the hem of Quin's jacket and yanked her backward. She screamed as a young woman with purpling skin and varicose veins reached for her face with all the grace of an adolescent going in for her first kiss, mouth wide open. Quin slapped her.

Quin had a decent amount of first-hand experience with zombies, no thanks to Fergus, but his thralls had been, well, dead. Expressionless. Dull. This one went through several phases of emotion in quick sequence: annoyance, confusion, anger, hunger, hurt. It was queasily familiar, unnervingly alive.

Bess slammed the butt of her snapbow hard into the zombie's head—who released its grip on Quin—unintentionally firing off the quarrel, which sailed out of sight. As the undead woman stumbled back, Bess leveled her bow to shoot, only to realize the quarrel's absence. As the zombie pitched forward, a bolt buried itself in her right temple and she fell hard to the ground, motionless apart from a twitching ring finger. "Watch it," Jenny grunted with creepy, wide-eyed stoicism as she lowered her bow to reload it. "Bess, sweetheart. Breathe. *Breathe.*"

"Oh my god. Oh my god," Bess said, face sweaty with terror. She stared down at the zombie. "Anne, I'm so sorry, I'm..." She tore her bright eyes away to Quin. "You...you alright?"

"Fucking look all right?" Quin barked. Something dripped down her forehead. She wiped at it and her fingers came away with some kind of black ink on them. She nearly retched. Blood. Zombie blood.

Moving. She needed to keep moving. The zombie with the bolt in its head was already starting to stir. Quin broke back into a light jog, as jogs went, and the two watchwomen easily kept pace behind her. "Look. If you're...if you're a witch," Bess said, voice warbling with fear, "can't you just, I don't know, do witchy things to them? Change them back? Please?"

Quin flushed. "Don't be stupid." But truth be told, nothing had ever stopped Quin from practicing necromancy or zoimancy. She'd just hadn't gotten around to either of them yet. Or any of the other magical disciplines among the planet-spanning list of things she'd been blissfully procrastinating on.

As the Crescent loomed, the zombies' behavior changed, slowly but noticeably. They went from lone wanderers to pack hunters, traveling in close-knit groups of five or more, banging their fists against wooden doors, battering them down and shambling into the homes of screaming prey. Some boosted one another through windows, onto balconies, onto the dilapidated overhead bridges crossing the streets.

Quin was as impressed as she was horrified. Zombies were supposed to be solitary and stupid by nature. Just walking hypothalami, really. If she hadn't known there was a Xalic vampire involved, Quin would have made a mental note to kill Fergus at the first opportunity. Necromantic power of this scale and precision was too dangerous to let run wild.

Speaking of. Down the street, the vampire was riding on the Flaming Nip's broad shoulders, jutting out her freaky second jaw and making some kind of ear-grating noise. It sounded like two goats fucking, with a bit of a demonic warble brewed into the call. The Nip's nips farted out tiny spurts of flame in tempo.

The vampire was singing, Quin realized. Some kind of preternatural parody of Fergus's zombie-raising song—gnarly, wet vowels twisting themselves into a braying aria. The vampire flapped her arms about in apparently random patterns, conducting the slaughter to fit her desired rhythm, the zombies before her responding to the commands and running around, small children frantically trying to follow a parent's contradictory orders.

And Fergus was nowhere to be seen. Fantastic.

"At least she's distracted," Quin said. "Let's go, Fergus isn't—"

"She who? That?" Bess said, gesturing to the vampire. "What *is* that?"

"Long explanation short, evil little magic-stealing bloodsucker," Quin said. "But she's not the major issue here. Well, she *is,* but we can't do anything about it until we find Ferg—"

"So this is all happening because of her?" Bess said.

Quin cleared her throat. "Well, let's not point any fingers, but sure. Now come on, let's—"

Jenny stepped up alongside her and aimed her reloaded bow at the back of the vampire's skull.

"No, idiot!" Quin screamed, lunging for the snapbow too late. The string cracked and the quarrel buried itself in the vampire's head, knocking her off the Flaming Nip's shoulders and dropping her seven feet onto a rare patch of paved road. She lay still in a rapidly blooming pool of obsidian blood.

"Oh God Alfurious, please be fucking dead," Quin prayed.

For a few blessed seconds, it looked that way. Then the tiny vampire pushed herself to her feet and ran a hand up the enormous gash in her skull. It was like watching a magician's act—the blood, bone, all evidence of a wound, vwhup! Gone. The vampire picked out Quin's little group, crossed her arms and tapped her foot at them with teacherly disappointment.

"That usually kills people," Bess said through a hard swallow.

"Usually, yes," Jenny agreed in a hoarse whisper.

The vampire pointed at them, her second jaw popped out and she let out a sound that made Quin's guts curl into themselves. Like the kind of cry coming from a mother who'd just watched her child's skull get crushed by a passing carriage. Every zombie within listening distance turned on them, bloody drool dangling from ravenous red mouths.

They dashed straight at them.

"Run!" Quin shrieked.

"Where?" Bess shouted.

"Fucking anywhere!"

The zombies closed in. Quin let out a terrified scream and bolted toward the Crescent. That, at least, was made of stone and was easily defensible.

Assuming the place was emptied of zombies by now. If it wasn't, well, then they were right and truly buggered.

She ducked as she heard crossbows going off behind her, looked back and wished she hadn't. An entire crowd of undead was stumbling in her direction, and those two beautiful, brave morons had drawn their figurative line in the sand and were opening fire. Good. They'd buy Quin a little more time to get away once the zombies swarmed them and gnawed them down to their—

Curses, where are we even going?

Quin skidded to a breathless halt as a headless Fergus wobbled out of the Crescent's front entrance, his cloth-covered neck tossed across his back. She pulled the long white sleeve off his face, revealing the bastard beneath. Draped as he was, he looked like a fleshy, blinking feather boa. *Ah, she returns! Lovely to see you, Quin. I'll try not to hold your failure to rescue me against you.*

"Your head's off!"

Most kind of you to notice. I once again made the fatal mistake of putting my trust in the fairer sex and am currently reaping the rewards. I'm sure you can sympathize.

Quin gripped his rubbery neck with two hands and whammed his open throat down on the stump like it was an obnoxious groundhog. She held it there with one hand, snapped her fingers on the other and backed off. For a moment, Fergus's head hung limp, then he bolted upright as much as an ostrich could be upright to begin with and gasped like it was the first breath of his life, completely healed. *Ah! Oh, that was strange.* He examined himself. *How in the blazes did you do that? You don't have any of your...oh, you little pettifogger! You can use magic without tools. You can, can't you?*

"Shut up, Ferg." She rooted through what few pouches were still strapped to him. "I...need...my musket...shit! Where are they, Ferg?"

What, what are you looking for?

"My balls."

Pft. Say again?

"My musket balls!"

Ah. Try the one closest to my tail. Just so you know, it's possible they were taken by those cabal of priests you left me at the mercy of back at—

"Got one!" She yanked out the most beautiful ordinary orb of lead she'd ever seen. "Ferg, you know how to load a musket?"

He twisted his head around to face her. *You don't?* he asked with vague amusement.

"I wouldn't be asking if I did, Ferg! I need you to show me."

All right, all right. No need to squawk. What do you need to know for, anyway?

Quin's eyes damn near popped out of her head. "What do I..." She gestured to the zombies, back to him, to the zombies. "Eh? Eh? Eh!"

He eyed her suspiciously. *How can I be sure you're not going to shoot me—*

She gripped his throat in both hands and squeezed. "Because when your time comes, Fergushar, I plan on making it protracted and deliciously fucking painful."

Promises, promises, said Fergus. It was difficult, on account of his telepathy, to tell whether she was succeeding in strangling him.

Quin shrieked as something backed into her and loosed her hold on Fergus. But it was just Bess, retreating to load another quarrel as the horde bore down on them. Beside her, Jenny had run out of bolts and had drawn a vicious-looking dirk. "Have you loaded your gun yet?" she asked with a hint of urgency as she slashed at a zombie's face and took off its nose.

"Into the Crescent!" Quin shouted as all four of them began to retreat.

Ah, no, I would advise against that, Fergus said. *Last I checked, there was still a fair few zombies in there.*

"Then where do we...get back here!" Quin screeched at Bess and Jenny, who were retreating into the Crescent. Bess had drawn a sword and was hacking and slashing inefficiently at the growing crowd of undead that were encroaching on them. Jenny had somehow procured a whip and was lashing at the crowd with it, but what good was something like that against creatures that had no sense of self-preservation and felt no pain? Jenny—or was it Bess—let out a bloodcurdling war cry as they came to the Crescent's gates, vanishing beneath a tidal wave of zombies.

"No!" Quin cried.

Well, they're dead, Fergus said matter-of-factly.

Heart thundering, Quin looked around wildly for somewhere, anywhere to go. She needed time and space to load her gun, but more and more zombies were bearing down on them. Couldn't go back into the colosseum, couldn't set up any kind of defensible position. Couldn't run into a house for cover—who knew how many undead would be lurking inside? And the longer this went, the more people would die, the more zombies would be created, and the greater Quin's chances were of dying painfully in a hail of sticky, searing white flame, courtesy of the Queen's own.

But beggars couldn't be choosers.

"Ferg, kneel," she said.

Fergus made a face like she'd just asked him to gargle latrine water. *I beg your pardon?*

Quin kicked him behind the right knee and Fergus squawked in pain as he collapsed onto the other, grunting as Quin clumsily vaulted onto the saddle on his back and nearly slid off the other end. The stirrups were too short for her legs, so she leaned forward and wrapped both arms around his chest, clutching onto him and her gun for dear life. "Ride, asshole! Get us back to the hotel so I can load this thing in peace. Go!"

If I weren't so very fond *of you, Quin,* Fergus snarled as he shakily rose to his feet, *I'd buck you off in the middle of these rotting cretins and let them feast on your fetid—*

Quin screamed absolute bloody murder at him, every single filthy, vile curse she knew to spur him on. And it worked, the bastard finally bolted off down the street, negotiating the sea of undead with relative ease, jerking leftward and rightward and shouldering his way through the corpses. Quin held on for dear life while desperately trying not to drop her gun. She looked back to make sure the vampire's army wasn't running after them. Thankfully, they'd left the ghouls in the dust. If Quin had looked back to see hundreds of undead zipping after her, she probably would have shat herself right there and then.

Quin?

"Urghagh?" Quin grunted, not daring to speak for fear of biting off her tongue.

Some directions on getting back to the inn, if you'd please.

* * *

Her name is Brand, Fergus explained with a faintly urgent stride as Quin—sitting on her mattress—carefully poured the oddly sweet-smelling yellow gunpowder into the barrel of her musket, just as he'd instructed. His father had taught him how to shoot, and he'd occasionally gone on hunting expeditions with the man, along with members of his political cabinet. Sometimes to bring back game. Sometimes to clear out the cabinet.

The zombies hadn't yet reached the *Royal Hospitality,* but Fergus had a feeling they'd get there sometime soon. For now, the two of them were holed up in Quin's room, and of course, her accommodations were significantly more upscale than his had been. She at least had furniture. The priests had gotten a bucket and some matted furs that looked like they could stand on their own.

Fergus went on, *She didn't say much, figuratively speaking. But from the sound of your description, she is indeed a Xalic vampire.*

Quin gave him a murderous glare as she spat out another small mouthful blood on account of her bitten tongue. "And you used necromancy right in front of her. Good going, Ferg. You've pretty much gone and killed a whole town."

Meh. Wouldn't be my first. Besides, I'm sure they'll bounce back. When I was the Death Lord of Jocrom, towns I purged with zombies usually became quite the popular hotspots for tourism. But if I may digress on that point, I have a query. As you saw earlier, I survived and maintained consciousness after having been quite expertly decapitated. Did that have something to do with your magic?

Quin kept mum.

I'll take that as a probable yes. While we're on the subject of your abilities, I've never seen you shoot this gun before. Is it some kind of witchy gun?

"Bravo, Ferg. It goes with my witchy jacket and my witchy boots."

Fergus glowered at her. *Don't patronize me, witch. You're the only one of those I personally know, but you've never been terribly open on that front. Or in general. About as much as a nun's legs, I'd say.*

Quin sniggered. "You and I have met very different nuns."

Evidently, he said, trying very, *very* hard not to picture Quin engaging in writhing, sweaty coitus with some foul, pimpled, frock-swathed abbess. *The gun,* he insisted.

Quin started ramming the rod down the gun's barrel. "It's a witchy gun, you got that right. And if I'm going to believe the old bags who gave it to me, it should either disintegrate...what's her name again? Brand? Down to nothing, or it might backfire on me and blow a crater the size of Basdolon."

Fergus swallowed. *Odds on the former?*

"I don't know, a solid eighty-twenty, maybe?"

That's not good enough, woman.

Quin yanked the rod out of the gun, threw it on the floor with a loud clack, stood up and got in his face. "Don't whine at me, Fergus," she snapped. "You've got no right. This whole thing?" She pointed a finger dangerously close to his beak. "*Your* fault."

I fail to see how anything I've done could possibly be construed as anything less than—

"Shut it. I don't want to hear another word out of you." Quin motioned for him to move aside from the doorway, which he did. Then he fell in-stride behind her, but she whipped around and pointed a finger in his face. "No. You're not coming."

I hardly think—

"I'm aware, Ferg. And I don't need you fucking things up more than you already have."

Fergus drew himself to his full height, which he quickly regretted once he banged his head on the low ceiling. After a few cranial shakes to clear the stars from his eyes, he deepened his voice and said, *I am Fergushar the Tenth, Death Lord of Jocrom and Soltan of the Pale Star. For all I respect you, Quinolyn—*

Quin's face turned the same color as her hair. "Fergus, you are *not* endearing yours—"

—You quite frankly will not be able to solve this particular rumpus—

"Rump...wha... You're underselling it by a country mile! People are dead!"

—without my assistance, as I am the most premier necromancer in the world, so I am singularly qualified to help—

"Esder's going to fucking dissect me for this, you twit!" Quin said, her voice laced with a singular, genuine terror he found himself, quite curiously, unable to enjoy.

Fergus took a step closer to Quin until he was looming over her. *Silence, wench!* he roared to shock her out of her feminine delirium.

Quin went silent, trembling with fury and terror.

Thank you. Now. Without my help, you will undoubtedly be unable to overcome Brand, should your aim be untrue. Therefore, I'm choosing to disobey. He lowered his head so the two of them were at bulging-eye level. *And one more thing. Never, ever*—he punctuated each "ever" with a stab at the air with his beak—*assume to command me, Quin. Again. I respect you, but*—

She leveled her gun at his chest.

Well, that wasn't the reaction he'd expected to his gracious offer of assistance. Then again, when were women ever predictable? Fergus eyed the open barrel, conspicuously pointed at his heart, and didn't feel quite so Soltan-like anymore. *Um, Quin?* he said, backing up a few steps. *I would greatly appreciate it if you demonstrated basic firearm safety and*—

"Do you know why I keep you around, Fergus?" she said in a low, distressfully calm tone that didn't quite match up with the crackling tempest in her eyes.

He blinked. *Erm, pardon?*

"You heard me just fine."

I...well, regarding the precise reason, no.

"Go on. Guess."

Is this really the time?

The hammer went *ca-click* as she cocked it halfway back with her thumb. "Humor me, shitweasel."

He wasn't sure he liked where this was going. The loaded magical musket being aimed at him besides. *Well...I always presumed it might have something to do with my charming disposition. That or you were hoping to pick up a thing or two about necromancy.*

Quin's face twisted into a nasty sneer.

I'm, ah, guessing I'm a bit off the mark?

"Oho, yeah," Quin said. "Wanna know *really* why?"

Well, again, I'm not sure this is the best of—

But Quin didn't seem like she intended him to get a word in edgewise. Her voice had gone whisper-hoarse, and every word was a fresh drop of acid burning through the tumbledown floorboards. "The only reason I haven't blasted your worthless carcass into chutney and sent your consciousness to an eldritch dimension to be repeatedly scoured until you go mad from getting bored of it is because I. Couldn't keep. My fucking. Mouth. Shut."

Fergus searched for a witty retort. *Uh?* he managed.

"When I told Her Majesty what I'd turned you into...shit. Shit!" Quin lowered the gun and slapped a hand to her head and let out a strangled, laughing chortle. Then an ear-grating, girlish squeal of an impression of Her Resplendent Majesty exploded out of her: "'Oh, what a fabulously marvelous idea, Quin! You've given him an opportunity for redemption! To turn from his evil ways! Oh, I cannot *wait* to see what you do with him!'" The false mirth fell from her face. "Fuck only knows what becoming an ostrich has anything to do with redemption. Fuck only knows how anyone could possibly think *you* would be worthy of it."

Well. Hardly as if he could argue against that.

"I had to play babysitter until the Queen thought you turned over a new leaf. She put it in writing and everything. And I couldn't change the terms because the damn thing was boilerplate. Seriously! She's got pre-made forms for dark lord guardianship. Who in the fuck thinks to have something like that prepped?" Quin huffed like she'd just run a marathon, red-faced and scowling at him.

Until now, Fergus had consoled himself over his sorry state with the hope he'd finally found someone who, well, liked having him around. To hear otherwise was uncomfortably disconcerting. But in a way, this revelation was simultaneously comforting. The status quo was maintained: He was still a lonely wretch, yet he commanded power. After all, he had one of the Five Witches of Incolf at his whim.

He couldn't show weakness to this trollop, otherwise he'd be chum in the water and she'd smell it. *So...as long as I don't inadvertently loan my power out to magic-stealing vampires and wipe out half a town's population, we're fine? Did most of those people really count, anyway? I mean, they were poor. Who knows? I give it two weeks, tops, before the local economy realizes substantial improvement.*

The look Quin gave him almost convinced him all that caterwauling about other dimensions and something-something supremely nasty torment might not actually have been girlish bluster. Then he finally caught onto something: *Ah. By the by. You made a grammatical mistake. You said 'had' to play babysitter. Not 'have.' I'm shocked at you, Quin. As a writer, you ought to have a firm grasp of...*

She was giving him a wide-eyed, crazy-looking, toothy half-grin. Waiting for the ball to drop.

Oh. I'll take a guess that I'm truly the one with egg on my face here, then?

Quin slashed a hand through the air. "We're *through*, Ferg. Forget crossing the line, you've jump-roped it. You're getting one chance. Once Brand's dead, you'd better be a hundred leagues from here, because if I see you again—"

You'll destroy my soul, explode me into stardust, blah blah blah? Fergus frowned. *Hang on. If you really had that much power, why haven't you used it yet to take care of Brand and the rest of the—*

Quin flicked her gun barrel, motioning for him to start moving down the hallway. The conversation, apparently, was over.

And for whatever reason, that simple gesture impressed the situation's reality into him. She was really telling him to go. And God only knew why, it actually hurt.

He scoffed at himself. Companionship was beneath him. With a dignified flick of his head, beak turned purposefully upward at Quin, he walked away, down the hall. *Bird or not, Quin, I'm the Death Lord of Jocrom. Powerless I may be, I still have my exquisite brain. No matter where I go, I'll be running the place in no time flat. You are foolish to be letting me walk free—*

Quin slammed the door hard enough to jostle dust from the ceiling.

It was like a spell had been broken, and his mood suddenly turned. The figurative manacle was removed from around his leg. He was free! No more enduring her constant harping about how he couldn't kick passing peasants or explode granaries or peck children who looked at him funny. No more having to stick around that squalid printing hut back in Basdolon and listen to journalists going on about non-issues like political bribery and abuses committed within the church.

Fergus sauntered downstairs, strolled through the now-thoroughly trashed front lobby and kicked the door open. It broke from its hinges and slowly fell into the street like a drunk who'd finally succumbed to one-too-many. He strolled through the now-abandoned streets, sighing happily, reveling in his freedom, dancing in the thickening downpour. The screaming of widows and children though, he could do without. Couldn't they quiet down, for just a few minutes? It wasn't like their wailing would save them.

As he strode through the rain, marching through the squelching mud all the way to the town's front gate, he wondered where he'd go first. What other nearby towns were there where the local constabulary and political apparatus was made of gelatin-brained nincompoops? It was a ridiculous question, the answer was obviously "everywhere." His lack of ability to speak though, that was going to be quite difficult to circumvent, no matter what degree of intelligence the local officials retained.

Fergus stopped as it hit him like a kick to the groin. Right. He was still an ostrich. And Quin, perhaps the only person on the planet capable of restoring him to humanity, was planning on heading straight into a swarm of zombies. With a gun that— her being a woman and therefore incapable of properly handling a firearm—probably hadn't even been loaded right. And she'd forget to keep it covered from the rain, he had to bet.

Bother.

Fergus rushed as fast as the foul, muddy morass that was Queensworth's pathetic roads would allow, straight back to the *Royal Hospitality*. But when he got to Quin's room, the door was wide open, and she was gone.

Oh. Fergus' knees went weak, and he lowered himself to the floor. *Oh, damn it.*

A floorboard creaked in the hallway.

Fergus shot to his feet. *Quin!* He poked his head into the hall. *Thank God—*

The zombified innkeeper trundled up the stairs, mouth still connected to jawbone by a few spindly strands of tissue, blood mixed with spit dripping onto the floor. His pale purple eyes locked on Fergus, and he slowly shuffled toward him, arms outstretched.

Ah. You're not about to try and eat me, are you? Because from the look of it, I think you'd have a hard time managing. Good Lord man, what'd you do? Deep throat someone's foot?

The zombie was halfway down the hall now, and Fergus was of a mind to run for it when the zombie held his hands up to his face, like someone had just shoved a torch in it. Except the zombie was making the gesture toward the space where the floor met the wall. There was something lying there. With trepidation, Fergus carefully emerged into the hall and crept toward whatever the foul undead was cowering from.

It was about a hand's length, black and shriveled. It looked like a banana peel...no, not a banana peel. The foreskin of Urg the Erudite!

Fergus looked at the cowering zombie, then the foreskin, back to the zombie. He kicked the desiccated prepuce straight at the innkeep, and as the shriveled member skittered across the floorboards straight in the zombie's direction, he made a sound almost like a scream and stumbled back, waving his arms like he was trying to ward off a sudden onslaught of long-separated aunts.

Fergus grinned. *What's wrong, friend? You have something against dried peener?* He kicked the foreskin at the zombie again and got the same reaction. He kept it up until the zombie was at the edge of the stairway and finished the job with a hard kick, sending the innkeep tumbling down the stairs. There was a loud crack as it hit the bottom, and its knee poked out from somewhere it wasn't supposed to. *Ha! That's for putting me up with those God-bothering creeps, you miserly little wretch.*

How providential was it, for the priests to have cast this particular talisman aside. Assuming the innkeeper's reaction wasn't from him harboring a fear of pricks from when he'd been alive, the last remaining piece of ol' eloquent Urg could perhaps keep Fergus safe from the rest of the undead. He could assist Quin with it. Maybe even bring harm to Brand!

Fergus pinched his newly recovered equipment in his beak and carefully placed it in one of his few remaining pouches. He'd gotten fairly good at that over the last few years. He'd had to, having no hands and all.

He traipsed down the stairs, hopped over the zombie, ran through the open door and into Queensworth's streets, which were accumulating even more zombies. Though if Fergus were being honest, if it weren't for their mauve-recolored eyes, he would have had a hard time telling the difference between Queensworth's populace from yesterday and today.

Now. To business. The way he figured it, Quin would go off looking for Brand. And Brand would be wherever there were the most undead. Which would probably be back the way they'd came, toward the Crescent.

All right then, Quin. You better be grateful for this. Fergus ran off to rescue his reluctant confederate from whatever doom awaited her. Overhead, the rain stopped, which he took for an omen of his inevitable success.

Five, Four, Three

Quin, holding her hotel bedquilt over her head for crude shelter from the downpour, was halfway across the damp plank serving as a bridge from the roof of one squat, two-story townhouse to the next when she realized it had stopped raining.

And the zombies, in turn, noticed her when they heard her boot come down on creaking wood, no longer masked by the downburst's crackling roar. A dozen of them stared up at her. Some of them pointed at her and made a noise like Brand's wail, but softer. The message was clear: We see you.

"Shit!" Quin threw the quilt away and rushed to the other side of the plank. The moment she was on solid, flat rooftop, she pushed the plank bridge away, letting it crash into the street below where it pinned two unfortunate zombies. No chance of them following her anymore. But when Quin looked for the next bridge, she realized there wasn't one. And this particular townhouse was too far away from any other building to have needed one. She tried the double-door hatch leading downstairs. It was locked.

She'd trapped herself. "Oh, fuck me," Quin groaned as she kicked a puddle. "Good going Quin. Real smart move, real smart."

She crept toward and peered over the edge of the townhouse's wide but pathetically short parapet, which must have been built to keep mice from falling off, because she couldn't imagine what else it was good for. A shudder ran down her spine as dozens of undead looked up at her at once. She scuttled a solid seven feet back.

Very, very trapped. How was she supposed to kill Brand now? Just hope and wait for her to come by? She needed to lure her out. Again, how? Quin knew nothing about hunting vampires. And she couldn't afford to wait around. The longer this took, the more likely it was that word would reach Basdolon and the Queen's counselors would send some Sunspots to clean up the mess. Quin pictured being covered in their sticky, bone-white flame and shuddered.

But the minutes dragged into hours, and nothing came to her. Quin found herself lying down on the still-damp parapet, gun tucked beneath her on the roof's surface. She reached out to her typewriter in Basdolon. She had to do something, even if it didn't help anyone. Keep herself occupied.

She began typing up a new page.

```
The Conflagration of Queensworth…
```

Quin's hands paused where they hung in the air, fingers curled skyward in vague approximation of where her typewriter's keys would be, as if it were dangling directly above her. She wiped a finger across the sky, erasing the text. Had to keep the vocab at a solid primary school level.

```
The Burning of Queensworth went on
for hours. The ravenous flames roared
as    they    ate    their    way    through
barnacled   clusters   of   concentrated
rotten  wood,  clogging  the  air  with
smoke   drifting   northward.   Darkness
fell and the clouds parted to reveal
```

```
the sea of stars. Its lone island:
the moon, blindingly bright—hanging
like   a   lamp   illuminating   the
spreading death below.
People screamed. Parents wailed for
their   children   in   increasing
desperation. People cried for their
friends, their families, or they did
it because it was the only thing they
could. The panicked shouts of the
city watch, trying desperately to
figure out who was in charge and why
they hadn't done anything yet, were
buried beneath…
```

Quin scrubbed her thumb across a smoke-obscured star, erasing the last two lines. Her fingers brushed the pads of her typewriter's keys, but the queasy feeling in her gut kept her from writing more.

The screams finally began to die away. Now, the air was alive with the moans and sighs of the tottering undead, exhausted and hungry. She could pick out the voices of children among them.

A voice in the back of her mind whispered to her: "Your fault."

Quin bit her lip and started a new page.

```
Your Majesty,
I hereby tender my resignation as a
member of your court. Signed, your
humble servant Quinolyn Schumacher,
Fifth of the Five.
```

No. She crumpled the paper into a ball and tossed it aside. She could almost hear it landing in her apartment waste bin, a perpetual waystop for half-baked confessions of fuck-uppery. If anything, Siobhan the Third ought to be the one apologizing to *her,* saddling Quin with Fergus instead of letting her disintegrate him. He'd been nothing but trouble for her since, and now look where this stupid little experiment on "redemption" got her: stuck on a roof while hordes of the undead prowled.

Redemption. Blah. There was no redeeming Fergus. How many undead had he set upon his neighboring kingdoms, blighting the earth with the loose guts and shit they'd left trailing in their wake? How many children had he fed to their undead parents before throwing them into Jocrom's moat as a warning to any potential invaders? How many centuries back did he send feminism in that wonderful bastion of culture he'd turned into his own private drug den?

She should have killed him the day Jocrom fell.

It would have been so easy. She could still feel the soft silk of his robes in her hands, hear his bleating as he prayed to his entire pantheon for divine intervention, see him waving his skinny arms as she dangled him over the parapet of his castle's highest tower. All she'd had to do was open one finger, and he'd have fallen into the morass of the dead and dying packed like sardines into the courtyard below, one half screaming, the other mostly silent as they fed on the screaming.

But no. Instead, she'd had to go and turn him into a telepathic bird. The whole ostrich thing had been something of a joke between her and the rest of the Five, one of the few things she'd ever genuinely bonded with them over: Wouldn't it be absolutely delicious to take some overcompensating little twit and turn him into the one land-based bird known for having the largest...

Quin raked her cheeks with her fingernails. Damn it all. She'd been sixty-eight years old when she'd transformed Fergus. Young for her kind, sure, and youngest of the Five, but it wasn't like she'd matured slower than ordinary humans. As cliché as the sentiment was, she should have known better. What good had come from Fergus's protracted humiliation? How had her stupid, spiteful decision benefitted...

Quin sat up. The Five. That was an idea. And if she had any others, it would have been the very last on her list.

"Shit." Quin sat up and took a stencil out of her jacket pocket. She drew a window-sized box in the air with it, and it trailed a glowing blue line behind with each stroke. Once she finished drawing the window, the stencil disintegrated.

Quin grabbed at the air within the box's area. The rooftops beyond creased and folded like she gripped a patterned blanket, and she tore them away. The floating abyss before her was black and filled with stars.

The strain kicked in. Skin prickling, sound fading. Drawing this was one thing, keeping it open was another. The longer she kept it up, the worse the drain would get. "I, Quinolyn of...fuck." She didn't want to do this. Forget spending her magic, talking to the other four was about as enjoyable as a tooth extraction. Dumping a problem on them? Tooth extraction by way of a rusty spoon.

She probed her brain for *any* alternative, no matter how desperate, and came up short. "Fuck. Fuck, okay. Deep breath. Deep breath." Quin took that deep breath. It did about fuck-all. Nothing else to do but soldier on, then. "Okay. I, Quinolyn, Fifth of the Five, call upon Johanna, Third of the Five."

She waited for the space to fill with a wizened face. Nothing. "Johanna, I call upon you." Still nothing. Quin stomped her foot with impatience. "Hanna, you crusty old fart, answer the damn—"

"Not *now*, Quin," hissed an old woman's contralto before it grew in volume. "So, when we get to chapter four, we're going to take a look at the origin of humiltublist ore, and how it became integral to the development of the city's infrastructure during the thirty-fifth century..." Johanna's voice began to fade.

"Hanna, I *really* need to talk to you." Quin worked her jaw to find the hated word: "Please."

The pause felt like it took years, but the sigh at the end of it was worth the wait. "I'm sorry everyone, I need to step out for a minute. You can start on chapter two while I'm gone. I'll be back in five." And the way she elongated "five" was as clear a message as any. Quin heard heels steadily clacking down a hallway, and in a few moments, Johanna appeared before her, standing alone in what looked like a broom closet.

The Third of the Five's tan, bullshit-weathered face was long and thin, with a sharp nose and sharper gray eyes, and she'd let her long, thick silver dreadlocks fall where they may. Today, she was dressed in a double-breasted suit—lemon-colored, of course—paired with a white shirt, hands folded behind her back.

"Alright, Quin," said Johanna, as if Quin were an estranged sibling who'd come home begging for money. "What is it?"

"What?" Quin asked with a forced smile. "I can't just call every now and again? How's the Galvinhame weather treating you? I'm sorry about the 'crusty old fart' bit, by the way."

Johanna checked her wristwatch. "If you want to beat around the bush for another four-and-a-half minutes, Quin, that's your prerogative, but I'd appreciate it if you stopped wasting my time and let me get back to my class." Her tone gentled, just a touch. "So why don't you just tell me happened?"

Quin baked as much reticence into her tone as possible. "Well, I went to Queensworth to do an article, and long story short, now there's a zombie outbreak." She made sure to cringe a bit to earn just a smidge of pity points. "With a Xalic vampire serving as field marshal."

Johanna looked at her in that I-can-see-through-you-down-to-your-molecules way. It made Quin shiver. "Fergus?"

"Um. Yeah. Fergus."

"Figured as much. Well, I'll say this for you, my dove: You're lucky Her Holy Majesty's not her mother. Siobhan the Second would've had you pincushioned with a hundred snapbows if you stuck so much as a toe back into Basdolon."

"You, ah, won't say anything to her, will you? Siobhan Three."

"Are you serious? Of course not. She'd never manage to keep that to herself. And the absolute last thing I want to do is go all the way out there to explain to her congress of butt-kissers why you don't deserve to be burned at the stake." Johanna groaned and dragged a hand down her face. "Quin, you have to stop making more work for us. We can't keep covering for your mistakes. I'm going to have to call on Esder and tell her what's happened."

Quin swallowed. Esder. Something deep down was urging her to tell Johanna what she'd learned, about her and Medina and the whole thing. But she held back, afraid Johanna already knew. Worse, she condoned it. And all the implications stemming from that little possibility were so astronomically awful Quin resolved not to think about it for at least another few days. Assuming she lived that long.

"She'll probably want to talk to you about this," Johanna said. "And I know you and I will absolutely be having words the next time I'm in Basdolon."

"But..."

Johanna gave her a penetrating *Don't-insult-me I-can-tell-this-is-somehow-your-fault* look. Quin winced. "Look, Hanna. I'm sorry, all right? Sincerely. *Please* don't call Esder. I'm trying to fix this; I just need some advice. How'd you track down vampires, back in the day?"

Johanna ran a hand through her hair and sighed. "Vampires, vampires...I just found whatever creepy castles were around and destroyed them. Does Queensworth have any of those?"

"No."

Johanna gave an impatient shrug. "Then I can't help you. Good luck, Quin." She raised a hand and pinched an unseen fold in space, pulling on the patch to close it.

"Wait!" Quin cried. Johanna paused, looking increasingly annoyed. "I need to lure her out so I can shoot her. You have to tell me, how do I do that?"

Johanna sighed as if she'd just been asked to get off the couch and wash some dishes. "Give her something she likes, probably."

"Like what, a fucking bouquet? You're not helping me, Hanna. Please, *please*, I need some kind of direction on what to do here, before the whole town goes to the dogs." Which it honestly already had, but acting otherwise at least let Quin hope.

Johanna pursed her lips and stroked her chin for a few seconds. Then she snapped her fingers. "All right, here might be something. So what you could try—"

A sensation like someone had just driven an icepick up her nose hit Quin so hard and suddenly the whiplash threw her onto the rooftop's surface. She curled up into a twisted ball and shrieked as something chewed its way through her frontal sinus.

Then the pain faded as fast as it had come. After sitting up and catching her breath, she looked at the void and wished she hadn't. Where Johanna had been was now a painfully beautiful woman who, like Quin, looked significantly younger than she actually was. She'd been blessed with sharp cheekbones and close-cropped coal-black hair standing out against ivory skin. Her viciously sharp jade-green eyes looked like they could bore through bone.

"Five," the Fourth greeted her with the hoarse whisper of someone who had been smoking hashish pipes for the past three hundred years. Which she had, and no degree of youth-granting magic could conceal that. From the look of it, she was inside a moving carriage. She wore a long, shimmering bathrobe of baby-blue satin hugging her svelte frame. The light danced across its scaly patterning.

Quin uneasily stood, too terrified to be angry or indignant about the trespass into her mind. She managed to pry the words out of her throat, "Um. Hello Esder."

"You're in Queensworth?" asked her fellow witch.

"Yes." Shit. How did she know?

"With the zombies." She said it like she was halfway through reading a shipping ledger.

She knew that too. Dear god, *how*? "What?" Quin said with a nervous laugh, feeling the sweat gather on her forehead. "Oh no! No zombies here. None at all."

Esder leaned forward, one eyebrow raised. "A pigeon came with a letter. Declared zombies."

"Nope! Pigeon's...pigeon, really?" She waited half a heartbeat for Esder to crack a smile and give away the joke before she remembered just who she was talking to. "Well, pigeon's totally full of it. No zombies here! Everything's fine." Quin forced a grin.

Esder frowned. "Hm. Interesting. We were informed—" Her image flickered a few times and froze.

"Esder?"

After about half a minute, Esder's face came back into focus and motion. Her expression had been placid, but now she had the sort of exhausted, silently incandescent look parents reserved for their children when they want them to know just how much they regret their conception. "Johanna confirms zombies. You are the cause."

"I—"

"Liar."

Quin flinched. "Well, I mean, technically. But it was really Ferg—"

"Currently en route. Best run."

Quin felt a dull and heavy dread crash into the pit of her intestines. "*You're* coming to Queensworth?"

"With three Sunspots and two battalions. We've departed the rail station."

Sunspots. Quin swayed on her feet as a cold, sickly mal rushed through her. "But—"

"Goodbye."

"Wait!"

Too late. The image vanished, leaving Quin alone with the knowledge certain death was, at most, five miles away and closing.

Quin jolted as the roof's hatch blew apart in a spray of shrapnel, and the Flaming Nip stomped backward up what sounded like a wooden ladder, with Brand the Xalic vampire riding on his upper chest. Her hands yanked on the ears of his tipped-back head like she was using them to steer. The Nip gave Quin an upside-down snarl.

"Holy shit!" Quin snatched up her gun, but her thumb slipped off the edge of its hammer as she aimed. "Fuck!" She pulled it back with a whole hand, felt it click. She lined up the sights with the enormous gladiator, his pilot, and the entire conga line of zombies in the process of climbing up after their master.

Quin felt the gun's protective crystal crackle as she squeezed the trigger on a weapon she'd once leveled a mountain with.

* * *

For the love of all that was holy, how could it be so difficult to track down a red-haired witch and a vampire riding on a seven-foot-tall half-naked gladiator?

Fergus had spent what felt like all night searching this miserable town for his targets and couldn't find head nor hide of them. Now he was damp, cold, tired, and ravenously hungry. At one point, he'd considered heading back to the Crescent to glean leavings from the bleachers, willing to overlook their foulness. Then he considered some of those leavings might include people-bits and decided he could deal with a grumbly tummy for a little longer.

At least he had no trouble seeing anything, as he had the moon's glow and firelight to guide him. He had to admit, he was impressed Queensworth hadn't completely gone up in flames yet, though the rain probably had a hand in that. At least he could see long ways down the street and know if he was walking toward a crowd of zombies.

And annoyingly, he had yet to do that. Everywhere he went, all he could find were paltry groups, not the crowds he'd been searching for. If she were smart, Brand would surround herself with as many undead as possible. It's what he'd used to do, back in the day, to protect himself as he rode into conquered cities.

When he'd turned what felt like his thousandth corner that night and nearly run headlong into a solitary zombie with its back turned to him, staring silently and statue-still up at the moon, Fergus stomped in frustration. *Shoot! Blast! Crud! Sod! Minger! Agh!* He kicked mud at the zombie with every curse.

It turned, and he found himself facing a woman with her head lolled to the side, because half of her neck was no longer there to support it. Her swollen belly protruded through a matron's uniform. Her flesh was still blessed with the warm, pallid glow that would, in the coming hours, turn blue, then black at the fingers as her blood congealed, before finally falling into decay. It was almost beautiful, in a way. Like watching a neglected tapestry rot over the years, the intricate patterns coming undone at the seams, unwoven by time. Just faster and with flesh.

Fergus winced. *Ooh. Sorry about that. Didn't notice you were with spawn. Congratulations, by the by. Quick question: I don't suppose you've seen a vermillion virago with a magic peashooter?*

The zombie stared.

A red-haired woman with a gun.

The zombie stared.

Right. Well. Could you perchance point me in the direction of your master? He hadn't really expected that to work, but to his surprise, the zombie raised her arm and pointed westward. *Why, thank you! Much appre—*

The zombie raised her other arm and pointed southward.

He sighed. *Well, you're no help at all, are—*

When Fergus was ten years old, his father had taken him up to the very top of their palace to show him their kingdom and their subjects. He remembered looking down into the streets of Harashin, watching as thousands of multicolored ants zoomed through the streets with the efficiency of a well-oiled machine, whole groups marching in near-perfect lockstep, maneuvering their way through traffic with a hypnotizing fluidity. Fractals intercepting and penetrating each other without ever truly touching.

But more vividly, he recalled looking down and feeling some kind of funny tingling sensation travel from his bunghole up to his spine and make a parabolic, lightning-fast descent into his gullet.

The polluted Queensworth air crackled with the same vertigo-induced nausea for a half-second, and the whole world seemed to suck in a breath, creating its own pregnant pause. It was a moment in a nightmare, that sudden, intentionally dramatic freeze directed by a half-asleep brain to warn the captive dreamer the drooling wolf *was* about to leap and rip them apart. A perverse, hairs-on-the-back-of-the-neck warning.

His stomach heaved, his feathers stood on end, every inch of his skin prickled in dreadful anticipation. Everything went dead-silent, apart from Fergus's soft, *What in the...*

He shrieked as a tiny, static discharge snapped at the tip of his beak. And with that, the primal fear that had been worming its way through Fergus violently expelled itself as a toot of wind. It better have been a toot.

He couldn't help but feel let down, and very, very confused. *What in...what in the blazes just happened?*

The pregnant zombie didn't answer. Instead, she was now staring north by northwest, just a few degrees shy of the Crescent. Fergus looked past her and spied another zombie just down the street, looking in the same direction.

That couldn't be a coincidence. He ran in the direction they were staring, toward a sector of buildings looking impressively tall and well-made for somewhere like Queensworth.

He finally came to a townhouse where a large crowd of zombies crowded around, and they were all staring at the roof. And blocking the entrance. As Fergus approached, their heads snapped toward him in unison. Slowly, they began to march toward him, carnivorous intent plain on their drooping faces.

Filthy mongrels beware, Fergus said, suddenly feeling quite brave. Perhaps it was their lack of weapons, or their lack of any cognizant thought that would otherwise allow them to cooperate and concoct a strategy. *You face Fergushar the Tenth, Democratic Emperor and Death Lord of Jocrom, Soltan of the Pale Star, Thorn in the Side of the Fifth of the Five—eugh, that rhymed—Wizard Extraordinaire, Necromancer of Great Power, Host of...of...bah, the Great Birdly Todger, why not. Whose powers have no equal, and whose glorious legs can deliver a kick with two-thousand pounds per square inch of force. And you're all between me and my ticket back to humanity.*

He looked up toward the roof where he figured Quin probably was. *At least, I hope so. And if not, oh well. I'll have fun killing you all again either way. Have at thee!* Fergus hurled himself into the awaiting morass of decaying flesh.

Crucial Conversations

Bugger mother and bugger her fucker, who knew a tinny click could be so utterly heartbreaking? Quin's misfired musket drooped in her hands, and its magic crackled and faded into the wind, along with that perverse, electric anxiety it had bled for an awful, but mercifully short stretch. She would have bashed the weapon to pieces against the brick parapet out of frustration if she weren't about to get the same treatment by a gigantic half-nude gladiator and his inversely sized pilot. Both of them were advancing on her like she owed them a sharp degree of interest on a loan.

"Shit shit shit!" Quin shouted as panic flooded through her. She fled to the northwest corner of the roof and checked over the side, desperately searching for a quick exit and cursing herself for not bothering to look harder for one earlier. No fire escape, misplaced ladder, pile of garbage, nothing. Nowhere she could jump. Just a guaranteed three-story descent toward a broken neck.

The southwest corner. She dashed in that direction and a row of zombies blocked her, a mangled and silent wall, dozens of arms intertwined and just as many legs spread. When she tried to juke one out and duck underneath to make her escape, several kicked at her. One bare toe clipped her chin, and the shock more than any actual pain sent her reeling back.

Zombies closing in in a half-circle, a gladiator-riding vampire taking up the other flank, and behind her, a deadly drop. Cornered. "Oh, come on," Quin whimpered. This couldn't be it. This couldn't be how she died, for god's sake. She desperately tried to weave a plan for *any* way out.

Nothing. Squat. She was fucked. Quin shut her eyes and her whole body went rigid with tension, fingers curled into tight fists. She waited for the end.

A few seconds went by. A few more. Quin wondered what the hell was taking them so damn long and dared to crack open an eye.

They were all still there, staring her down, dashing her hopes that maybe they'd spied something more interesting than her on the other side of the street and had silently made their exit. On top of the Flaming Nip's trunk-like, veiny neck, Brand was squinting at her.

"Uh," said Quin. Only now did she realize the feeling like someone had tied a rope around her midsection and was gently tugging her in the vampire's direction. And all she had to do was loosen her stance, lower her resistance, and her magic would be gone. Siphoned away. Quin tensed her physical and metaphysical self.

Which didn't prevent the cold touch of her own magic as it penetrated her mind. Brand's "voice" was two in one: a righteous, clear-toned vibrato, mixed with lingering traces of Fergus. *Pardon me, young lady. If you don't mind my asking, what's your name?*

Quin flinched, reeling from the introduction of yet another voice in her head. "M-my name? It's, ah, Quin. Quin Schumacher."

Brand tapped the fingers on one hand against the Flaming Nip's cheek, looking like she was considering something. Then her mouth fell open, a pink morass of gum and blood. *Goodness! I think I know you! Were you the woman who wrote the article that shut the Basdolon Hound Derby down? Quin Schumacher?*

The flattery of recognition took a bit of the edge off of Quin's still-lingering fear she was about to be devoured. "Oh, ah, yeah. Yeah, that was me." And that article, coupled with the Derby's closing, had caused such a stink the only way to stymie the stream of angry letters dumped into the *Stardust's* mailbox had been for the front office to demote Quin from investigative journalist to colosseum critic.

Oh, thank you! Brand said.

"Uh. For what?"

Why, for the article!

"Oh, ah, sure. Why?"

Because what those ruffians were doing to those dogs...oh, my heart! Disgusting. Absolutely shameful and disgusting. That place needed to go to the dogs. Brand snorted. *Forgive me, that wasn't intentional. By the by, do you know if those poor pups managed to find good homes?*

"I, uh, think they did, yeah." In all honesty, Quin didn't know or care, but whatever the vampire wanted to hear, she'd tell her.

Good, good, I'm glad to hear it, Brand said, still wearing a faint smile as she waved a hand at Quin's discarded gun. *If you don't mind my asking, there's a lot of magic coming off that gun.* She leaned her head back and sniffed. *Actually, there's a great deal of magic coming off of you. Old-time magic, smells like. So, I'm just wondering, what's a reporter doing with that kind of...* The friendliness in her expression melted into an adversarial sneer. *Esder? Is that you?* She latched back onto the Flaming Nip's ears and squeezed them. His hands curled into fists. *Are you on another one of your tricks?*

"What? No! No, no nononononono, I'm not Esder," Quin said, frantically waving her hands in front of her. "Definitely not Esder! You think Esder would go anywhere near somewhere like Queensworth? She hates being dirty. You know what she did once? When she got a bit of dirt under a fingernail, she cut the tip of her finger off and let it grow back instead of just cleaning it out."

Slowly, Brand relaxed, and she let out a half-hearted chortle. *That does sound like her, come to think of it. And Esder isn't the sort of woman to resort to disguise. So how do you know her, if you don't mind my asking?*

"How do *you* know Esder?" Quin said, though she had a feeling she knew the answer.

Well, I do believe I asked you first. So if you'd oblige me, I would greatly appreciate it.

"We're, ah...sorta in the same line of work."

Brand looked gobsmacked. *Journalism? Really?*

"No, um...witchcraft."

Oh, I see. Then you're another of the Five. That's the magic I smelled off of you. She licked her lips. Quin swallowed, but then confusion worked itself into Brand's expression. *But that can't be right. Your scent, it's like...well, honestly, it's not very strong. If you don't mind the comparison, you're just one rose. A dry one, at that. Esder's more along the lines of a whole garden. Verdant. Pruned.*

"Oh. Sorry?"

No need to apologize! Honestly, that was rude of me. Please accept my apology.

"Erm. Sure. Accepted," Quin said. "Ah. You wouldn't happen to be a member of Her Majesty's government, would you?"

Brand made a face like she'd been slapped. *Indeed! That's quite sharp of you. How could you tell?*

"Because I interviewed Ben Medina last night. He told me everything." Though "everything" was stretching it. His notes had mostly been a depressing chronicle of how he'd survived Queensworth, light on details implicating Esder. There was at least enough to convince Jack and the other *Stardust* editors to let her keep digging.

Again. Assuming she survived and all.

Ah, Ben, Brand said, sounding mournful.

Quin hissed through her teeth. "Is he..."

He's passed.

"Oh." The vampire didn't elaborate on the how, and Quin decided not to pry, and to ignore the guilt twisting her stomach into painful knots. "You knew him?"

Well, on a professional level, yes. We both worked at the head office.

"So...you were a member of Her Majesty's cabinet?" Quin found that hard to believe, because Esder would never allow a vampire anywhere near the queen. Maybe she'd been a lower-level employee?

Brand grimaced. *As much as it shames me to say now, yes. I was.*

"Doing what?"

Well, I was the M-Double-I. For two terms.

The Minister of Immigration and Integration. Quin's jaw dropped as she realized who she was talking to. "Holy...you're Ylena Koring!"

Brand's face registered more than a little surprise. *You know me?*

"Yeah! Well, not personally, but we reported on your disappearance, and...good lord, that was five years ago, now I think about it. Where've you been this whole time? And why're you calling yourself Brand?"

Ylena worked her jaw, and if Quin squinted, she could maybe see her doing the same for the second one. *It's my stage name. And to answer your first question, I was here. Was it really five years?*

"Yup. Here in Queensworth?"

Yes. In the Crescent, always.

Quin licked her dried lips. "Because of Esder."

Ylena spat a fat, bloody lob over the side of the building. *Because of Esder. She carried out the deed, but if you want the root of it, you can look at Her Majesty.*

Quin let out a disbelieving laugh she swallowed when Ylena's expression stayed furious. "The *Queen* sent you to the Crescent?" That was ridiculous. Quin knew Siobhan. The woman was next to harmless. Sure, she'd put the occasional maid to the whipping post, but...all right, maybe she wasn't past sending people she didn't like to a fighting pit. But she was always so sweet. If about as bright as a dying candle.

Well, while I'm not one to make assumptions most of the time, I'm confident she signed off on it, Ylena said. She stretched her neck and pointed to a patch of skin just below the right side of her jaw looking like it had been attacked by an army of vicious squirrels. Right where her carotid artery was. *See this? I was put in a cell with a Xalic vampire. Morriss. He fed on me and died the day after in a bout. The transformation was...well, terrible's putting it mildly. But at least it got a lot harder for the other contestants to harm me. However, I couldn't live long without a steady supply of food—blood, I mean—I either earned in the arena or was supplied with from Crescent management. So, I couldn't leave.*

Quin almost asked why she couldn't have fed on the local populace and gone north toward the rail station, but decided it would probably be better not to give her any ideas.

With a tug of the ear, the Flaming Nip reoriented himself northward, toward Basdolon. Ylena shook her head. *I was sent here and so were many of my colleagues. I've had to listen to them die. Watch them be ripped apart.* She poured steel into her voice. *But now I have the power and the muscle to avenge them upon Her Majesty.*

Quin maneuvered herself in front of the Flaming Nip, but out of strangling range. "Why would the Queen send you over here? You know how powerful she is? If she wanted you dead, you'd be dead."

I have wondered about that, to be honest, Ylena said. *Because she needed to manufacture plausible deniability, perhaps? Maybe she wants to do away with Congress. It wouldn't surprise me if she sent the others off to other colosseums. The Entraillion, the Whirligig. It would be a smart move, barbaric as it is. You could keep the local entertainment sector going and get free evidence disposal in the bargain. And you can't get any help from the crowd, tell them who you are. Your tongue's gone.*

Quin pointed at the Nip. "He's not a politician too, is he?"

Ylena didn't appear to have heard her. She looked down at Quin, righteous fury sparking behind her eyes, which flickered between white, black, red and purple. *Mark this. Her Majesty and her government haven't heard the last of me, oh no. Not when I have this much power.* Her eyes flashed a deep purple. *The most I've had my entire life.*

Ylena gave Quin an apologetic look. *But it's not enough, Schumacher. Not to take on Her Majesty. Or your fellow witches. Besides.* She gave a sad, sidelong look to the assembled zombies standing nearby. *The people of Queensworth, bodies and souls ripped apart. I have to make it worth it. I need more.* She looked back to Quin. *Every drop I can find.* She let out a sad, if somewhat insincere-sounding sigh. *I'm sorry. You don't seem like a bad young lady.* She kicked her heels against Flaming Nip's mighty mammaries. He reached out for Quin.

Panic shot through her. "Wait, wait wait wait!" Quin shouted, heart pounding painfully. The Nip's hand froze. "We can work something out! There's, there's a compromise here, has to be! We can figure this out."

Ylena's lips set themselves at a line. *Are you willing to abandon your oath and help me overthrow Esder and Her Majesty's government?*

"Well, ah, don't you think that's a little drastic? I mean, we'll have to do a little more digging—"

The Nip started reaching for her again.

"Wait, wait!" Quin shouted, fighting the overpowering urge to do something stupid, like try for her gun again or to hurl herself off the roof. She slapped at her coat pockets, looking for it, where was it...there! She whipped out her *Daily Stardust* press ID. Wasn't sure why, as she'd already said she was with the paper. The emphasis couldn't hurt. She showed it to Ylena. "I can get you down on the record like Ben, send a story to my editors. We'll get this out to the people. Everyone in Incolf will know what Esder's done, what the Queen's done."

Ylena snorted with disbelief, but Quin saw something in her face. An unspoken "What if?" she was doing a piss-poor job of hiding. Serious consideration, a dash of hope. *So you won't take up arms against the Queen, but you'll still write critically of her? Most people would still consider that an act of betrayal, you know.*

"I wouldn't be betraying anybody. I'd be getting the truth out into the world."

Ylena scoffed. *Once I've taken over the city completely, Her Majesty's finest will be deployed here. Once they're under my power, I'll have more than enough of it to spread the word on my own. I won't need a tabloid's help. No offense.*

Shit, Quin had forgotten about the approaching army. "They're already on their way. Esder told me. She's coming with some Sunspots."

Ylena sighed. *Nice try.*

"Wha...I'm not lying!"

I'd like to believe you, but it seems more likely you're saying whatever you need to save your own skin. Because you were going to say we need to flee next, correct? That I need to survive to tell my story? You'd be saving yourself in the bargain. But I don't blame you. I'd do the exact same thing.

Honestly, Quin was having a hard time seeing beyond her own terror—of having her magic drained or getting turned into puddle of fried goo, and it was hard to decide which one would be worse—but that bit about telling Ylena's story was a good idea. "Come on, Ylena. What've you got to lose here? You're telling me you wouldn't even let a paper with half a million in readership carry your story?" The skin under Ylena's eye twitched. Quin saw the cracks in her defenses widening. "You can tell me everything on our way outta town, all right? What's the harm? If I'm lying, you still get your story out there, and hey, I'll even see if I can get more of the *Stardust's* staff to look into it. If I'm telling the truth, which I *absolutely* am, we dodge the Sunspots. Do you really want to take the risk?"

Ylena tapped her fingers against the Nip's nose. *How can I be sure you are being truthful here, Schumacher? About anything?*

A good question, because she wasn't. Not completely. *The Daily Stardust* maybe went out to thirty-thousand readers on a good week, and the story's likelihood of being published—now the Queen was directly implicated—was next to nil. But Ylena didn't need to know any of that.

"You'll just have to trust me. All I can say. We can get going on this, at least." Quin brought out her pad and pencil. Better to use a writing implement her subject could actually see, instead of her distant typewriter. "I can jot things down. What do you say?" She held her breath.

The hours she'd spent waiting up on this roof felt like a snap of the fingers compared to the time it took for Ylena to say anything. Eventually, *finally,* she gave an assenting shrug. *Well, all right. So, I just talk, and you write?*

Quin nearly crumpled in relief. "Pretty much," she said, licking at her salty, sweat-coated upper lip. "I've got shorthand down pat. Where do you want to start?"

Hm. Where would you recommend?

"At the beginning?"

That sounds agreeable.

"Then fire away. Before the Sunspots...you know."

Ylena sucked at her gums, looked pensive for a moment like she was weighing some options, then pointed southward. *Just for the sake of caution, let's put as much distance between ourselves and the north side of town as we can so—*

Hark, fiend!

Fergus, his white dress covered in gore, stood at the rim of the hatch with fury burning in his onyx-black eyes. There was something blacker and shriveled clamped in his beak—the Urg talisman. *Meet your doom!* He took a considerable bite out of the foreskin and swallowed.

As Quin clasped a hand to her mouth and heaved, Fergus charged straight at Ylena, halted in front of her, and spat a thick black glob of spittle right onto her cheek. She winced and massaged the Flaming Nip's earlobes. His meaty hand shot out and gripped Fergus by the throat. *You're still alive? What* was *that?* she said, rubbing the wet spit on her cheek.

Fergus's enormous eyes bulged from his tiny head as he made panicked squawking noises. *Did you...just...talk?*

Of course I can talk, Ylena said.

Why...didn't you...say....glck, Fergus choked, tongue desperately flailing out of his open beak.

Because, Ylena started. Her head imploded. Blood, brain, skull, vitreous humor, mucus, cartilage and god only knew what else erupted from the top of her head as the rest of it was crushed as if by a giant invisible hand. The moment her tiny body toppled off the Nip and hit the ground, the zombies' heads all went likewise. The Flaming Nip, the wall, all of them.

A spray of gore, they swayed on their feet, and all fell. Immobile. Definitively dead.

Quin stood statue-still; her face splashed with the same hot blood soaking her notepad. She watched as maybe the most important story of her career dripped onto the roof's gravel-spotted membrane. Her fingers went numb, and the notepad fell out of her hands, splashing in the widening pool of vampire and zombie blood. Which she had absolutely no idea how to vanish or dry.

She should've felt relieved, now that she wasn't going to be drained. But all Quin felt was a crackling rage at the feathery bastard before her.

Whew, said a freed, coughing Fergus as he shook himself, sporting the most smug, vile grin Quin had ever seen on a living thing. *Thank goodness I found that talisman. Could you believe it? One of my idiot captors had lackadaisically discarded it in the middle of a hallway. It's a good thing it never made contact with human tissue, otherwise we would have definitely been blown to—*

Quin threw her writing implements away and lunged for Fergus, wrapping her hands around his throat and squeezing, but it was too thick and muscular for her to strangle.

What, this again? Fergus snapped, sounding confused and annoyed rather than threatened, which only encouraged Quin to squeeze harder. *What did I do? Apart from saving your worthless carcass from the other worthless carcasses? A tiny dab of gratitude wouldn't go amiss, you know. Do you know how hard it was to find you? Well, actually, not that hard, down in the street they'd all stopped to stare at this particular—*

"You...ruined...my...story!" Quin snarled through clenched teeth, regretting oh so very much she kept her nails as regularly trimmed as she did. She could be burrowing them into his trachea right about now.

Fergus blinked in vague confusion. *How? You still got a sporting good show at the Crescent, thanks to yours truly. If it's any consolation, the schedule of Queensworth's last standing gladiator is wide open now for a well-deserved front-page splash. I can recount and regale the many traumas I endured today. Though I wouldn't count this among them, on account of your wispy upper-arm strength.*

Quin screamed, pushed him away and snatched up her gun. The wood gave a soft crackle beneath her white-knuckle grip. Once the sights lined up with Fergus's head, he went stone still. Sure, the gun had misfired, but he didn't know that.

"Give me a reason to spare you," Quin hissed. "Any at all. I *dare* you."

Fergus made a sarcastic wheedling noise somewhere deep down in his long, frustratingly thick throat. *Need I remind you I got decapitated today? And I got better? I think you'd be best off saving your shot. Besides, you're...what's that noise?*

Quin lowered the gun. She heard it too. A sustained note amplified several hundred times louder than its natural volume. She'd heard that sound—a single soft D flat blown through a gold-lined ram's horn—only once before: the day she'd turned Fergus. When the great walled city of Harashin, capital of Jocrom, was reduced to cinder.

"Oh god," Quin whispered.

A skyward whistle, a streak of white. For just a moment, the night sky gave way to daylight. Quin held her arms in front of her face to protect her eyes from the flash of light erupting from the Crescent.

She lowered them. The gladiatorial arena had been swallowed whole by a towering, bone-white flame spitting fireballs skyward and whipped its molten tendrils at any building in reach. Enormous palefire-cleansed stones sailed through the air, trailing smoke after them.

A shadow fell over her as a chunk of stony bleacher plummeted right toward where she was standing.

QUIN! Fergus cried.

No time to think of the consequences. No time to explain. She wasn't dying in Queensworth.

Quin snapped her fingers.

The chunk of the Crescent exploded into a cloud of butterflies, thick and orange, the color of the sun. Patches of light from the Sunspots' flame bled through their wings, like sunlight through a thick canopy of trees. Quin screamed and keeled over as what felt like an invisible hand shoved its way into her chest and tore out a piece of her heart. It'd been so long since she'd gone through this pain that she'd forgotten it and wished she hadn't. Then she could've braced herself for it.

Quin? said Fergus. She was almost flattered. She wasn't sure if she'd ever heard him more terrified than she did right then. Though of her or for her, it was hard to tell.

Quin groaned as she pushed herself to her feet and retrieved her gun, clutching a hand to her chest. "We...have to head for the gate, Fergus. On the way, you gotta tell me how to fix a misfire, the gun didn't..."

Quin, your hair.

She pulled a lock in front of her face. It was gray. And that wasn't the end of it—she could feel the changes everywhere else. Her bones were more brittle, she could feel the new pouches of drooping skin. There were bound to be other signs of aging. "Supposed to do that," she wheezed.

The townhouse shook beneath their feet as another chunk of debris crashed into a neighboring building, sending up a cloud of debris and searing flame. "The town gate! Move!"

Where—

"Down, dumbass! The way you fucking came up!"

But—

"Go!"

Fergus made for the hatch. Quin went after him, but it wasn't easy. Her stamina had already been low, but now she had the body to match her age. She was borderline decrepit. Slow, even with the threat of impending death to spur her on. And every careful step down the ladder made her joints burst in fiery agony.

She reached the bottom and tore as fast she could through a ruined living room into the streets outside, stumbling over the field of decapitated zombies Ylena had left for them. She accidentally kicked away something hard: a peg leg. Ben Medina's peg leg, coming to a clattering stop.

Another comet-like streak of flame flew through the sky and made landfall a few blocks down. A rush of superheated air crashed into Quin, almost knocking her off her feet.

Her racing heart pounded painfully in her chest as she desperately searched for Fergus. She didn't see him until he was suddenly all she could see, a beautiful feathery mass of filth. He knelt, and she thanked God Alfurious he still had the saddle attached to him.

Don't say I never stretch my neck out for you, woman. On!

She hauled herself into the saddle and clutched him tight. "Run!"

Fergus made like an arrow, hurtling through the streets. More white, star-hot fireballs roared overhead. An explosion on their right sent burning debris straight at them sidelong. Fergus ducked, swerved, kept going. Quin desperately patted out the small, natural fires blooming across his back. Survivors of the zombies were screaming, in the streets, in their homes. A naked man stumbled out of his front doorway, white flame eating at his flesh, chewing it away, letting greasy remainders drip at his feet. A girl fell off a roof, half her skin melted. Fergus nearly tripped over a howling dog trying to outrun its own burning tail.

Every breath was like taking in gulps of little glass shards. Quin's eyes were drowning themselves, her heart felt like it was going to explode. She smothered her face in her sleeve, waiting for the inevitable slowdown as Fergus finally had to start trudging through mud.

The heat intensified, a scorching bellow. The world was one furious roar, like hell itself was clawing its way to the surface.

Fergus's pace became faster, steadier. Quin looked down. The mud had been baked into brick.

She felt the biting at the right side of her neck and her shoulder became a searing agony, like someone was carving the flesh away with a knife. Quin screamed.

Your hair!

She snapped her fingers, making the follicles shrivel and die. All of them. The pain faded away, but her naked scalp still tingled like it was being eaten by angry fire ants.

Gate ahead! Quin picked her head up. There it was, Queensworth's front gate. Still shut. *How will we—*

It exploded open, pale flames burning the remnants away. One door fell from its hinges with a loud crash. Fergus cackled triumphantly as they stormed into the cool night air. Quin could still feel the heat licking at her back, but they'd done it. They were home free.

Fergus skidded to an abrupt halt. *Quin?*

About a half a mile down the road, at the lip of the dead forest, were hundreds of figures bedecked in golden armor. At their front were three bald men in yellow robes, using wands to trace glowing red runes into the air above their heads, forming great white fireballs that launched themselves skyward. They fell in parabolic arcs, landing within Queensworth.

And at the Sunspots' head was a solitary woman in a loose blue robe fluttering majestically in the breeze, arms folded behind her back. Quin ground her teeth at the sight of her. "Ferg," she wheezed as she uneasily dismounted. "Tell me how to clear a misfire."

He looked from the army to her and back a few times. For a moment, she thought he was going to do something stupid. Like ask her why she wanted to know. Or talk her out of it. *You're going to need some kind of pin or needle to clear the YOW!*

Quin plucked out one of his feathers, poking the end of the quill to check its sharpness. "Like this?"

In the absence of...well. Yes. That should work.

"All right. What next?"

She followed his instructions to the letter as the two of them marched their way to the arrived Basdolonian forces, coughing all the while, until Quin managed to get the gun ready again. Soon, they were a standoff's distance away from Esder and her merry band. A chill wind blew through the air. The Sunspots kept up their work. Explosions thundered behind Quin.

Esder looked Quin up and down. "You overdrew," she said with a clinical air. "Again."

"Put the fires out and get them to stop," Quin growled, indicating the sunspots with a flick of her gunbarrel.

Esder yawned. She walked forward until she was a few strides away from Quin. With every step, the grass burned away around Esder's feet, creating a sterilized stepping-stone path for her.

Esder sniffed. "No." She pointed a thumb over her shoulder. "Into the carriage. Now. We're going to talk."

Quin pointed the musket at Esder and narrowed the iron sights down until they captured everything below the skinny witch's knees. "Put. The fires. Out."

Esder cocked an eyebrow, maybe vaguely impressed. "I can go without—"

Quin cocked the hammer and pulled the trigger.

For a single instant, all the world was silent. Then a roar like the first breath of creation rang out for all to experience. A cloud of electric nausea swept in over the clearing like a tidal wave. Esder's army held their ears and wailed in pain, before doubling over and releasing their lunches. *God!* Fergus cried, collapsing beside Quin.

The Witch of Basdolon had just enough time to look surprised as the white, featureless Void yawned open where half of her legs and the ground beneath them used to be. She fell and caught the edge where ground met nothing, immaculately filed nails digging into the dead grass. It may just have been the first time Quin had ever seen Esder afraid.

Quin tossed the crackling gun aside and stumbled over to her senior. Groaning in pain as her joints flared up, she knelt and grabbed the elder witch by the front of her robe. With Esder grasping her wrists for dear life, Quin managed to unsteadily rise to her feet, holding the now-legless witch aloft, dangling her above the well-sized circular pit beneath them that was sucking in the air. The Sunspots trained their runes on the both of them and a dozen armored archers leveled their snapbows. Blood from the stumps of Esder's legs dripped into the white oblivion below.

Esder dug her nails into Quin's wrists in a desperate clinging hold, eyes wide with shock. "You..."

"Put the fires out now, or so help me," Quin snarled into her face.

Esder nodded and held up her right hand. Which crashed into Quin's face hard enough it might as well have been a straight punch, instead of the signal to the Sunspots Quin had been expecting. She fell onto her backside, stars swimming across her vision. When they cleared, Esder floated right above, her surprise washed away by placid calm.

With a couple clicks of her tongue, like she was summoning a dog, the earth closed in over to seal the Void away and climbed upward, forming a pair of lumpy legs for Esder. She ran a palm over each, wiping away the clay to reveal a fresh pair of legs, pale and sleek.

Her shimmering green eyes locked onto Quin's own and flashed rose-pink.

Quin gasped as she felt a pair of forceps being taken to her memory, delicately peeling the layers back for inspection. It was fast and efficient work, done in just the span of a breath. Above her, Esder's eyes pulsated angrily as a scowl set itself into her face. Which, for the barest second, was wrinkled and leathery, before snapping back to sleek youthfulness. "It *is* your fault." She eyed Fergus, huffed, and her eyes went back to normal. "You failed to keep a watch on him."

"I—"

"I'm forced to be here, dealing with this mess, on account of *your* irresponsibility."

Quin reached for her gun. It was spent, sure but she could at least take a swing at Esd—

The thin witch gripped the end of a pinkie and pulled, cracking a joint. Quin cried out as her shoulder popped out of its socket, invisible chisels finding the chinks in the rotator cuff. Prying and twisting.

Hey! Stop with...ooh. Fergus uneasily wobbled toward Esder and regained some semblance of composure. *Quit that! Nobody gets to seriously injure that woman but—*

"Stick your head underground until you need air again," Esder said, her voice layered several times over with magic, like dozens of her were speaking at once, each in a different intonation. Fergus eagerly bent over and burrowed his head into the dirt, tail-feather wagging happily for his trouble.

Esder beckoned toward her troops, and a group of men ran over with a stretcher, which they roughly dropped Quin onto. She tried to twist herself off, but the adrenaline keeping her exhaustion at bay had worn off. Plus, her shoulder really fucking hurt.

They marched her over to the frazzled company of soldiers and Sunspots, one of whom heaved as he bowed to Esder. "We've...agh. We've cleansed approximately three quarters of the city, my..." He belched and wiped a spot of puke from the corner of his mouth. "My lady. May we resume?"

Esder looked from them, to Queensworth, to Quin. "No. That's enough." She stuck a single finger up and blew on it, candle gentle.

The distant roar died out. Quin mustered her last drops of strength and angled her head to look back. Queensworth was no longer ablaze. It was quiet. Lifeless. Dark.

"Satisfied?" Esder asked her.

Quin tried to muster a colorful response, but her mouth was full of sand and her words were sinking into the back of her throat.

She sensed something coming, a foreign feeling like a warm, smothering blanket. It was cold and dark, yet queerly familiar.

Quin wasn't sure whether to laugh or scream. She coughed a faint, pathetic mix of both as, for the first time since joining the Five, she fell asleep.

Three's Company

Quin awoke in a tent. A pretty nice tent, by all appearances. It was plush and over-ornamented, with a hole at the top to let in the morning light. Or was it evening?

She was lying propped up on a plush ottoman, dressed in her usual clothes, albeit cleaned. Pages crackled at her five o'clock, and she recognized the thick wing-flaps of a broadsheet. Quin craned her neck to look behind her, which was more painful and difficult than she thought it would be.

Her eyes widened. Her Majesty Queen Siobhan the Third laid draped across a couch, swathed in long, flowing purple silks. Siobhan, like her mother, was tall, curvaceously plump, and wore her long, strawberry-blond hair in a skewered bun. Her vacant amethyst-colored eyes glided across a copy of the *Weekly Basdolonian,* that government-backed, typo-ridden shitrag. She flipped to the back, allowing Quin to read the front-page headline:

```
KITCHEN FIRE LEADS TO QUEENSWORTH'S
DESTRUCSION.
```

Quin had been out for a few days, then. Were they still around Queensworth? Or had she been shipped back to Basdolon to be cooked alive for the viewing pleasure of the masses?

A sharp, slick sound to her right. Esder sat at a portable desk that was buried under a carpet of tools—including, Quin noted with a nervous swallow, Esder's palm-sized derringer pistol. The

Fourth of the Five was hunched over herself and half-naked, covered from navel to forehead in glowing red runes she was carving into herself with a blue-feathered quill. Once she'd drawn the last rune in place over one tiny breast, she plopped the quill into an empty jar, pinched her sternum and pulled outward. A thin film of skin sloughed off her body, and the runes with it. Their light died out as she wrapped the translucent tapestry around a wooden tablet, then covered her raw, steaming pink skin with the blue robe bunched around her narrow, bony waist. She started fiddling with the runes, smearing them. Combining them.

Neither she nor the Queen had noticed Quin was awake yet. Splendid, because she was making a visible, retching effort not to vomit at whatever the hell Esder had just done. And because she wanted to keep herself frozen in this moment for as long as possible. She had a thousand questions she didn't want answered.

She probably wasn't a prisoner, seeing as how she'd been given such luxurious accommodations. But she couldn't shake the feeling she was definitely in the shitpit. Then again, they hadn't killed her. *But* she had to bet they'd come to Queensworth in the first place to destroy any and all evidence of what had happened to Ben Medina and Ylena Koring. So why not finish off the last piece of evidence?

Damn it all. Better to get it over with. Slowly, she pushed herself upright—her shoulder felt healed—and cleared her throat. Esder gave her a quick sidelong glance and a grunt of acknowledgment, but Queen Siobhan's eyes widened in childlike glee and she practically vaulted off of her couch and wrapped

Quin in a crushing hug. "Quinolyn! Oh, I'm so glad you're awake!"

"Your Majesty," Quin managed to wheeze, strangled by both the hug and Her Majesty's overpowering cheddar-scented perfume. Once she was released, she managed a half-bow. It just seemed like the polite and smart thing to do. "I'm honored by your presence."

"Oh, pish posh! Don't be so stuffy, Quin. Esder's got you covered there. Right Esder?"

"Auspiciously," Esder said.

"Listen to you!" Siobhan giggled. "Fancy words. Awes-pish-us-lee. You're a doll. Oh, it's too bad Fergus's not here for this happy moment!"

"Where is he?" Quin asked.

"Oh, he went off into Queensworth," Siobhan said.

"Unattended," Esder grunted.

"Oh, he'll be fine, he's a big boy!" Siobhan chirped.

"Unsupervised," Esder said, but her reproach fell on deaf ears.

Before Quin could ask what Fergus could possibly be doing in Queensworth, Siobhan chirped, "Oh, Quin! Esder told me all about why you got so old. So I gave you a little bit of a makeover! Take a look." She handed Quin a heavy silver handheld mirror.

An elderly, nauseous clown almost puked at her. Her tongue smacked at thick, clumsily smeared red lipstick. Blue eyeshadow threatened to cascade down wrinkled, sunken cheeks crudely painted over with pink blush. She'd been given a blond wig that had been done into pigtails. Fucking *pigtails*.

Esder cringed at Quin in apology.

"You're so pretty!" Siobhan squealed.

"Thank you, Your Majesty," Quin croaked.

"Oh, it was nothing. I've been practicing!" Siobhan let out a grating laugh that sounded like a pair of prairie dogs fucking. "I've had to, you know. My last makeup girl? She wasn't any good, you know. I saw her at the Entraillion. You know, she was actually really good there! I waved to her on her last round."

Quin slowly let the mirror fall into her lap at the mention of Basdolon's premier gladiatorial arena. "What?"

"I said I saw her at the Entrallion!" Siobhan shouted, like Quin had suddenly gone deaf.

"But *why* was she at the—"

Esder shot Quin a look that could have caused whole forests to wither and die, and Quin tried to return the sentiment, but then another wave of exhaustion hit her. Exhaustion and fury, as she realized all her on-record confirmation and testimony was now ash.

Of one thing she was certain: She wasn't staying in this tent another fucking minute. Quin looked toward the tent flap. "Thank you, Your Majesty, but I'd like to take my leave."

"Aw," Siobhan said, pouting. "You're going already?" Her expression hardened. "I *could* make you stay, you know."

Quin tensed, and tucked her fingers behind her back, ready to snap at a second's notice. She couldn't use her powers against the Queen—none of them could, by contractual obligation—but she could at least get out of the tent, give herself a head start. But it was also possible that using any more of her power would turn her into a pile of dust.

Then Siobhan exploded into a fit of giggles. "Just kidding! You can go, Quin. Oh! But before I forget." She rushed over to her couch and retrieved a tiny scroll of paper tied in a green ribbon that had been stuffed beneath a cushion. "I got this carrier hawk message from your boss. He said he needs you to write your first-hand account of what happened here as soon as you can!"

Quin took the piece of paper but didn't unroll it. Jack wanted her to write a first-hand account of what had happened in Queensworth? That meant getting interviews. "But...I can't..." she stammered. She couldn't write about this. She didn't *want* to write about this. All she wanted to do was find a grimoire of memory-erasing spells and try every single one.

"Oh, sure you can, Quinny Quim Quino!" Not for the first time, Quin was seized by the urge to rip her ears off and shove the closest sharp implement through the holes to carve that putrid string of nicknames from her gray matter. Though she'd be fucked if she were going to explain to Her Majesty why the middle one was so inappropriate. "You just have to believe in yourself! I have oodles of faith in you." The Queen gave her a big, beaming smile. Esder, for her part, went back to examining the runes arranged across her shed skin.

Nobody said anything for a while, and she let out a wide, thunderous yawn, Siobhan hopped where she stood and chirped, "Well, that's pretty much it. Nice seeing you, Quin! Oh, if you ever need anything from me, just let me know and..."—she assumed a dramatic pose and adopted a deep, dramatic voice— "...it shall be done!" And she laughed like she'd said something genuinely hilarious.

There had been ships at sea that had faced storms calmer than whatever was happening to Quin's face. It felt like her cheeks were trying to twist themselves into knots, in mutual relief and frustration. "Of course, Your Majesty," she managed. But when she tried to stand up, her knees buckled.

"Here," Esder said. She took the skin-wrapped tablet and tossed it into Quin's lap. There was a flash of light, and the tablet was either replaced by or transformed into a walking stick. Siobhan squealed in pleasure at the magic, but all Quin could do was smolder. Both at her situation, and at receiving Esder's unsolicited help.

"Thank you," she snipped as she took it and hobbled out of the tent. Damn it, suddenly she couldn't imagine life without this cane. It wasn't until she was outside in the morning light she got a better look at its head. It was, of course, shaped like an ostrich's. Cheeky bitch. Quin checked over her shoulder to make sure the Queen hadn't followed her out, and hurriedly threw the wig away. The rising sun—so it *was* morning—made her scalded scalp prickle.

Outside, an enormous war camp had been established. Siobhan's tent was at the end of a long artificial street lined with tents. Soldiers and other officials milled about, and up this road, many were coming in and out of Queensworth. The air smelled of ash.

Quin spied a moving cart covered with tarps. When a wheel hit a field stone and jostled it, something blackened fell out. A small leg.

She stared at it for a long while before she noticed Esder was standing next to her. Quin went cold when she realized the Queen was nowhere to be seen.

Esder wouldn't dare hurt her in front of Siobhan, but what about anyone else?

"Apologies for the makeup. She insisted." Esder wiped a hand over her own face, and Quin shivered as she felt an invisible one pass over hers. "There. Gone." Esder beckoned for her to come closer.

"What?" Quin said.

"Just come here."

Quin swallowed and uneasily crept forward, hoping her death would be quick. Esder put a hand on her head and tapped a finger. Quin howled as something wet and slimy sprouted from the left side of her head and fell down over her shoulder. She looked down, half-expecting to see her brain, and wasn't sure whether to be relieved at the sight of damp steel-gray hair instead. It fell down her shoulder in gleaming coils.

"The burned side may never heal. Again. Apologies." Esder gave Quin a long, hard look. "I smelled Koring on you. She's dead?"

Quin swallowed. "Yeah."

"You spoke."

"Huh?"

"You and Koring."

"We...yes."

"About."

Quin recognized the unspoken order to start spilling her guts. "She...said you sent her here. Or the Queen did. Ben Medina said about the same."

Esder clucked. "Yes. Her Majesty's orders. I saw it through. Both of them."

"Why?" Quin breathed.

Esder worked her tongue around the inside of her cheek. "Because Her Majesty asked me to."

"Again. *Why?*"

"I just said."

"But what about—"

"The rest of it," Esder said, in a condescending parental tone, "is none of your business."

Quin ground her teeth as her anger bloomed. "Then I'm going to fucking *make* it my business, understand? I'll write about what really happened. I'll make sure everyone from here to Galvinhame knows. Chew on that, you...you...skinny beldam."

Esder yawned. "I might." She waved a hand toward Queensworth. "Go do your job. And keep watch on Fergus."

Quin sneered at her senior and began to hobble toward Queensworth. What was left of it.

"Five?"

The word was like a spell, and Quin's bravado wavered as she realized she'd just insulted someone—rather childishly—whose power exponentially dwarfed her own. She whirled around, but Esder was gone.

Quin gasped as a hand gripped the back of her neck and pushed her head downward. "You *ever* let anything like this reoccur," Esder whispered into her ear, breath a series of frigid kisses that smelled of rotting flesh, "you *ever* give that fool another chance to do harm to our country, and I will rip out a thread of your soul and cast it into the Void. You will live forever knowing a part of you is missing. A hunger you will never sate. An anxiety you will never alleviate. And once you are dead, what's left of you will spend eternity scouring the entirety of existence for that measly, pathetic strand.

"Tell me, weakest of us, that you understand."

"Yes," Quin snarled, frustrated tears brimming at her eyes. God, how she wished she were stronger right now. Physically, magically, whichever.

The grip vanished. Quin collected herself, then checked her surroundings. No Esder. Just the wind, rustling at tent canvas and carrying the putrid stink of charred and rotted flesh to her. She stood rooted to the spot, images of Harashin flashing before her eyes. If she squinted, Queensworth almost looked like the ruins of Fergus's home. Quin forced herself to move and tried not to let the smell pull her back to that day.

Once she was out of the camp and trudging her way toward Queensworth's gate, she finally opened the letter from Jack. He'd written in thick black ink:

Hey Quin,

Went and picked up your article from your place, as arranged. Figured you stopped short because of all that happened. You'll have to tell us more about it, because the trains are blocked and all we've heard is what's come down the grapevine and the drek those lying twats in the Weekly Bee are printing.

Have to say, I'm massively into this new style you've got going on! Lotta grit, lotta pizzaz. You been holding out on me? Where was this kinda stuff for the Hound Derby?

Write something up about what really happened in Queensworth in this same style. I think our readers will get a real kick outta this.

Hoping you're okay,

Jack

Quin looked from the letter back toward the Queen's tent. They'd read this, but they weren't bothered by it? By the possibility she might actually get the truth out?

Maybe Esder didn't care. She probably didn't. And why should she? She'd faced down dragons, gods, and if the rumors were true, seven decades of menopause. Any reasonable person would ask: What could harm *that*?

Well, Quin would like to see Esder try her luck against half a million terrified and pissed-off Basdolonians.

She limped back into Queensworth, scheming her senior's downfall, plotting and drafting all kinds of nasty exposés.

* * *

Esder walked back into the tent. "She's leaving." She cocked her head at the figure draped across the couch. "Was the makeup necessary?"

"Siobhan" splayed her hands out in a shrug. "In all honesty, probably not. But it's the kind of thing Her Majesty would do." She stretched the body's thick legs over the couch's edge and sighed. "Hope you weren't too hard on her."

"Define hard." She looked her senior up and down. "If you'd please."

"What?"

"You know."

"No, I don't. Use your words."

Esder worked her jaw. "I want to speak face-to-face."

"Come now."

"I insist."

"Siobhan" sighed. "All right. Give me a second here."

The Third of the Five stood up from the couch, walked over to Esder's desk and picked out the paring knife. She buried the blade in her throat and sawed. A thick, viscous yellow gunk that smelled of freshly juiced lemons poured out of the wound, dribbling onto her shoulder and racing down her arm.

"Head's up." The head rolled forward off from the neck.

"You're not funny," Esder said as she caught the grinning semblance of their sovereign and gingerly placed it face-up on the table. A thick, graying bushel of hair slowly birthed itself from the weeping neck stump, then a sweaty face emerged from the gaping throat-hole.

"Eugh," Johanna said, taking a breath and wiping the sweat from her brow. "Glad to be out. Its stuffy like you wouldn't believe in there, Esder. And it smells like melted truffles. She keeps it up with those, she's going to go the same way as her mother."

"Murdered by her favorite whore?" Esder said, confused.

"Fat."

"Ah."

"So," Johanna said. "The whole thing about the hairdresser or whoever should have Quin running in circles for at least a couple months. Which should give us time to figure out how we can disappear Her Majesty's opposition without the risk of starting city-wide zombie incursions."

"I'm still in favor of wiping Five's memories. Or killing her. The bird as well."

"Hey, if you want to spend another couple decades looking for the last point on our little pentagram yet again, be my guest," Johanna said. "Besides. Things go wrong, and she gets wise? Well, I don't want to risk spending the rest of eternity as an ostrich. Do *you* want to spend the rest of eternity as an ostrich?"

"No," Esder admitted. "We need to research the counterspell."

"You haven't just scraped it from Quin?"

"She doesn't know it. Nor how she accomplished the transformation."

"That, or she does, and she's managed to hide it from you," Johanna said with a faint smirk.

The skin beneath Esder's eye twitched. "Impossible."

"Yes, well," Johanna said. "At the end of the day, it'll be a lot easier on all of us to just let her run herself ragged while she tries to figure out what she thinks Siobhan's up to." She sighed. "Of all the things she had to be when she grew up. Had to be a journalist. But at least she didn't go into theatre. Or follow Lore on one of her silly social crusades."

"And the bird?" Esder said. "Do we have leeway there?"

"You tell me. You wrote that contract."

Esder sighed. "No."

"Well, there you go then."

The two of them stood in silence for a while, before Johanna said, "Have you figured all this out yet?"

Esder shook her head.

"Do you at least have a guess?"

"Three, but I see no point in conjecture. Or questioning Her Majesty's motives," Esder said.

"Ess, I dropped a *lot* to come out here because you asked me to. I had to file about a week's worth of paid time off. I'm going to have about two days of that left after this. Do you know how many time-stopping-stones I'm going to need to burn through so I can grade seven hundred papers on time?"

Esder rolled her eyes. "Fine." Johanna spread her hands apart, an unspoken invitation to start talking. "The first possibility is political savvy."

Johanna scoffed. "You're pulling my leg."

"No. I've always entertained the possibility Her Majesty is concealing genuine cunning. Though I've considered this from various strategic viewpoints and still fail to see the value in disposing of government employees in this manner. There's no pattern. No obvious benefit."

"Okay. So what else?"

"Prejudice. Koring was immigration czar and Medina wasn't Basdolon-born. I didn't look into the ancestry of backgrounds of the rest, as I figured that you are evidence enough against that theory."

Johanna blinked and shook her head like she'd just gotten a cup of cold water thrown into her face. "I'm not...I'm not sure what to say to that, but I would still look into the rest of them, if I were you. Just to be on the safe side. How many did she have you go toss to the lions, anyway?"

"Nine so far."

"Good lord. Good *lord*."

"Mm. The final possibility is, well, she does it because she thinks it's funny."

"I don't think the woman who thinks fart and poop jokes are the height of comedy would be able to appreciate irony. You said you had three ideas, right? So that's all you've got?"

Esder shrugged. "I have more important matters to devote my time and thoughts to."

"Then I guess this'll stay a mystery."

"Indeed."

Another pause passed between them. "Doesn't it bother you?" Johanna asked. "Doing...this."

"Elaborate."

"Serving an idiot. Sending people to their deaths? People who don't deserve it? Well, okay, people who *probably* don't deserve it?"

"No," Esder said without hesitation or elaboration.

Johanna looked like she wanted to add something, then thought better of it. "Okay. Is there anything else, Esder?" she asked.

For a moment, Esder considered telling Johanna that she had tried to read the bird's mind, and was met only with a dark space, devoid of any substantial thought or memory. She'd never seen anything like that before. It was something impossible. Something confusing. Something...frightening.

"Nothing of significance."

Johanna sighed in relief. "Great, then I'm heading home."

Esder cocked her head. "That wasn't in the arrangement."

"Oh, it wasn't? Well, that's just too bad."

"I will have to explain to Quin where 'Her Majesty' went."

"I'm sure you'll come up with something." Johanna stuck a finger to her nose and blew. A small red marble popped out of the opposite nostril, and she swallowed it. She twiddled her fingers in farewell. "In a while, Esder. You owe me an astronomical favor for this."

There was a sound like a sneeze, and Johanna vanished inside the faux-Siobhan, which collapsed and folded in on itself like a blanket, apart from the lump in its center. Said lump migrated to the open, still weeping neckhole. A yellow barn owl hopped out of the collapsed skin, spread its wings, and flew up through the whole in the roof of the tent and out of sight, leaving a modest yellow feather behind.

Esder picked it up, admired the quill's point, sat down, pulled a few bones and muscles apart and began carving hieroglyphics inside herself. Right as she finished drawing a reverse-ankh across her aorta, she looked at the feather again and blinked in surprise. It was no longer a large yellow owl's feather. Now it was small and black. It looked like it would come from something smaller. Like a sparrow. Or a finch. Maybe even...

A shrike.

Esder whistled. She'd been so focused on being the one doing the duping that she hadn't noticed she'd been getting duped herself. "Two," she said, vaguely impressed. When was the last time she'd been successfully tricked?

Esder decided that she'd reward her elder sister's guile by tracking her down and ripping her apart at a molecular level only after she finished her carvings.

Bird on Bird

Fergus put his baton away as he prodded the decapitated, well-done corpse lying in the middle of the street with his toe. Yet again, not a hint of movement, nor a speck of magic. No necromantic energy at hand. That made eighty-two.

Around him, the Queen's scientists and volunteer nurse corps milled about a town razed—burned down to its wooden, pathetically delicate skeleton. Old bones purged to make way for the new. Or it would have been right about now if he hadn't been so foolish he'd let himself trust and be betrayed. By a *politician*, no less! A nauseating thought.

He scanned the ground for another corpse to check, though he knew with Brand dead, it was pretty much impossible to siphon back any of his power from fallen zombies, whether or not their heads were still in one piece. But this was also a good excuse to get away from Siobhan. For his money, the woman had rented out her cranial cavity for a syphilitic hamster to control. If it weren't for the fact she was being backed by a secret cabal of Quin's fellow magic-miswielding battle-axes, he would've conquered Incolf long ago.

"Hey, it's the bird," a woman muttered.

"That does appear to be the bird, yes."

Fergus looked for the source of the voices and found them: A blond woman in desperate need of a bath, sitting on the edge of a dried fountain bowl. And slumped up against her, a dark-haired woman cradling a snapbow.

The guards! If Fergus could whistle, he would have. How in the world did these two incompetents manage to survive?

By the look of them, they'd certainly had an eventful past few days. The two blood-crusted women looked like they'd just trudged through several miles-worth of mud, and had their arms wrapped around each other's shoulders, drawing the other in close for the assurance of a warm body. His heart quavered at the heartwarmingly pathetic display of friendship.

But forget a desperately needed cleaning, they needed food before their cheekbones started puncturing skin. He was surprised they hadn't been helped yet. Perhaps they'd refused assistance from the Basdolonians? Wouldn't blame them there, considering they'd turned most of their home to ash.

Judging by the way they were eyeballing him while fingering their crossbows, they were considering desperate measures. Fergus put at least a quarter-mile's distance between them before either of them could act on any ideas, though exhausted and battered as they looked, he doubted they would have been able to hit their mark.

Just looking at them made *him* hungry, so he made his way back to the camp the Queen and her retinue had set up outside the city gates, just far away enough the smell of charcoal and burnt flesh was more of a mild irritation instead of a crippling odor. Thankfully, Siobhan's collection of tin twits knew he was under Quin's protection, and by extension, Her Majesety's. To them, he was nothing more than a pet, a curiosity to laugh at.

And laugh they did when he raided their buffet table, but they weren't laughing when he managed to nick an entire rotisserie chicken and flee with it behind Queensworth's useless protective walls. It wasn't easy, seeing as ostrich beaks weren't meant for porting about entire chickens.

Fergus found a nice, private spot and gorged himself on the rotisseried bird, ripping off peckfuls and swallowing them whole. What did actual ostriches eat, he wondered? He decided he didn't care and nibbled on more crispy, dead bird. Not enough salt for his liking.

By the time he was done, there was a significant amount of chicken left. He considered taking it back—oh, the looks on their faces!—but his thoughts drifted to another pair, more sunken and desperate.

The two guards looked positively flabbergasted when he brought them the remains of the carcass, and he laughed as he watched them tear into it like starving hyenas, ripping chunks off and stuffing their faces. Then he thought of the starving children from when they'd first come in to town, which put a bit of a damper on his mood.

To his own surprise, the sight of an aged, sickly looking Quin hobbling in his direction did nothing to lift it. He trotted over to her. "You're still here," she said. She'd somehow grown half a head of curly silver hair back, and the right shoulder of her jacket now sported a mean-looking black burn scar.

Of course. Did you expect me to flee? Me, Democratic Emperor and Death Lord of—

"Yes."

Meh. Fair enough. He noticed her new walking implement, and the shape of its head. *Nice cane.*

"Thanks. And fuck you." Quin's gaze drifted toward the guards, and she did a double take when she realized who they were. "Holy shit."

Indeed. And all things considered, they're in relatively good shape. Moreso than some people I know. While we're on the subject, why do you look like that?

"Like what?"

What do you think, woman? Old. Doddering. Enfeebled. The washboard said something about overdosing. On magic?

The sarcastic answer he expected didn't come. "Overdrawing," she corrected him. "Sort of."

Explain.

"Why?"

Because I'm curious. And because the Death Lord of Jocrom commands you, while I'm at it.

Quin's lips managed a slight curl. "What's the magic word?"

Fergus felt like smiling, for reasons he couldn't quite place. *Explain, please, Your Wrinkliness.*

"Oh, well. Since you asked *so* nicely, I'll give you a hint. You remember what happened when I turned you into an ostrich?"

What? No. I barely recall anything from that day at all, no thanks to you.

"Then you're outta luck, Ferg."

Oh, come now! You can't reward my freely given politeness with continued obstinance.

Quin's expression darkened. "You think I owe you anything, after all *this*?"

Fergus huffed, but he took in the considerable encircling devastation once more. *I admit, I may have been a little imprudent with my powers.*

"Oh, that a fact?"

Yes, well. I make an oath, in whatever diminished capacity of a Soltan remaining to me, I will do better. Hopefully, that would placate her. He had no desire to be turned into a cloud of butterflies. They were not manly bugs.

"Not letting another magic-stealing vampire use your powers to slaughter thousands isn't that high of a bar, Fergus."

Well. Nobody's perfect.

Quin narrowed her eyes at him. Then, he saw it. Why she'd asked him about when she'd first turned him. He recognized that bemused, irritated glare. She'd looked *older* back then, when he'd been newly transformed. But in the time since, he'd just assumed he'd misremembered—one of the many traumas of his transformation. Because surely even witches didn't age in reverse. Though he supposed if they didn't have to age at all, it wasn't implausible.

So she got older when she used itemless magic. Or at least, it made her look older. Interesting. Now, he just needed to figure out how he could use that to his advantage and get her to turn him back. Perhaps if he procured a particularly expensive anti-aging skin cream before, she could start getting younger again. Or found a magical alternative. Then he could bargain for his return to humanity. Genius!

At any rate, Fergus said, *we should probably be heading back to Basdolon soon. I'm sure the* Stardust *is wondering about our safety, and I'm sure I'll have a considerable number of requests for my services waiting for me in our mailbox. Plus, we'll need to plot the recovery of my property from those frock-wearing n'er-do-wells you had me room with.*

"Yeah, we can't leave yet. Jack's got me doing an article."

Oh, come now. On what?

"Something about a town burning down."

Ah. Well. He stepped aside to allow her easier access to the pair of starving snapbow-women, who were finishing up the last of the chicken. *I believe I last saw these two shooting up a not-so-insignificant number of zombies. Perhaps they might go on the record?*

Quin looked back and forth between him and the guards, wearing an expression that implied accepting any help from him, even after everything that had happened, was not her favorite option. She scanned him with a paranoid glint in her eyes, looking for any reason to doubt him.

Then she gave an accepting shrug and whipped out a new pad of paper from her jacket. A mischievous gleam he didn't like shone in her eye. *Quin. Are you plotting something?*

"Ferg, how'd you like a job?"

If it means having to take orders from you, I'll eagerly and happily decline, thank you kindly.

"Even if it means getting to put one over on Esder and Her Majesty?"

Fergus considered that. *Does it pay?*

"I'll talk to Jack about it."

Then I demand an advance.

"Don't push your luck."

Well then. What is this job?

"Just go around town and find me more survivors. I'm going to need as much testimony as I can fit onto this pad. Track them down and let me know where they are. Bring them to me if you can."

Bring them how? Because I'm not doing any more piggyback rides.

"Lure them with food and water, I don't know. Just do what you can."

And how exactly is this supposed to 'put one over' on Her Legginess and Her Stupidness?

A vindictive, wretched smile crept onto Quin's face that made her look just a twee younger. "By showing them just how big of a pain in the ass a local paper can be."

Sounds to me like you're vastly overestimating the Stardust's *power.*

"Yeah, probably. But I'd still put it way above me."

Before he could inquire as to just whatever in the world that was supposed to mean, Quin went over to the two women and started talking to them. Fergus caught that one's name was Bess, and the other was Jane or something. If they recognized Quin, they were too tired to mention it.

Let me finish my work over here, then I'll get on it, Fergus called. Quin gave him a "Yeah, yeah" wave without looking at him, cane gripped between her thumb and palm.

While his companion chattered with her fellow members of the fairer sex, Fergus went over to another nearby body, this one with its head intact. It was a middle-aged man who looked like he'd had his guts torn out of his bunghole.

Fergus whipped his baton back out and pretended to tap a music rack. Just loud enough for Quin to hear, and therefore, to be annoying—but not enough to warrant a whack to the backside with that handsome-looking cane of hers—Fergus started singing his Song of Resurrection and conducting with his baton. After all, one never kn—

"DON'T YOU FUCKING DARE!" Quin shrieked at him with astonishing volume from where she stood, cane raised above her head with threatening implication.

Fergus yelped, ditched the baton and took off into the city's ruins to find her a suitable whelp to interview.

ACKNOWLEDGEMENTS

Thank you to everyone in the 17th Shard's Reading Excuses sub-forum who read the first draft and provided critical feedback. Thank you to William C. Tracy for having enough faith in the book (and its potential for profit) to publish it. And thank you to everyone who heard the title and didn't say what they were really thinking.

ABOUT THE AUTHOR

Jordan A. Werner is a Reddit-addicted bum who lives in the bowels of Southern California, just a ways away from the beach. He was born in Salem, ate his first lost tooth with a burger in Baton Rouge and once aced a spontaneous Beatles trivia quiz from a Trader Joe's bag clerk in Scottsdale, Arizona. You can find him at jwernerwrites.wordpress.com or on Instagram @jwernerdraws.

Please take a moment to review this book at your favorite retailer's website, Goodreads, or simply tell your friends!

www.ingramcontent.com/pod-product-compliance
Lightning Source LLC
Chambersburg PA
CBHW021550310726
48972CB00003B/759